MW01233136

The Certainty of a Future

Life in Mars

L. P. Gratacap

Alpha Editions

This edition published in 2021

ISBN : 9789354849121

Design and Setting By
Alpha Editions
www.alphaedis.com
Email – info@alphaedis.com

Contents

PREFACE BY EDITOR.

The extraordinary character of the story here published, which some peculiar circumstances have fortunately, I think, put into my hands, will excite a curiosity as vivid as the incidents of the narratives are themselves astonishing and unprecedented. To satisfy, as far as I can, a few natural inquiries which must be elicited by its publication, I beg to explain how this unusual posthumous paper came into my possession.

It was written by Bradford Torrey Dodd, who died at Christ Church, New Zealand, January, 1895, after a lingering illness in which consumption developed, which was attributed to the exposure he had experienced in receiving some of the wireless messages his singular history details. I was not acquainted with Mr. Dodd, but some information, acquired since the reception of his manuscript, has completely satisfied me, that, however interpreted, Mr. Dodd did not intend in it the perpetration of a hoax. His scientific ability was undoubtedly remarkable, and the facts that his father and himself worked in an astronomical station near Christ Church; that his father died; that his acquaintance with the Dodans was a reality; that he did receive messages at a wireless telegraphic station; that he himself and his assistants fully accredited these messages to extra-terrestrial sources, are, beyond a doubt, easily verified.

A mutual friend brought me Mr. Dodd's papers, which I looked over with increasing amazement, culminating in blank incredulity. On rereading them and considering the usefulness of giving them to the public, I have been influenced by two motives, the desire to satisfy the fervently expressed wish of the writer himself and the reasonable belief that if they are preposterously improbable their publication can only furnish a new and temporary and quite harmless diversion, and that if Mr. Dodd's experiment shall be in some future day successfully repeated his claims to distinction as the first to open this marvelous field of investigation will have been honorably and invincibly protected.

L.P. GRATACAP.

CHAPTER I

In the confusion of thought about a future life, the peculiar facts related in the following pages can certainly be regarded as helpful. Spiritualism, with its morbid tendencies, its infatuation and deceit, has not been of any substantial value in this inquiry. It may afford to those who have experienced any positive visitation from another world a very comforting and indisputable proof. To most sane people it is a humiliating and ludicrous vagary.

At the conclusion of a life spent rather diligently in study, and in association especially with astronomical practice and physical experiments, I have, in view of certain hitherto unpublished facts, decided to make public almost incontrovertible evidence that in the planet Mars the continuation of our present life, in some instances, has been discovered by myself. I will not dwell on the astonishment I have felt over these discoveries, nor attempt to describe that felicity of conviction which I now enjoy over the prospect of a life in another world.

My father was the fortunate possessor of a large fortune, which freed him of all anxieties about any material cares, and left him to pursue the bent of his inclination. He became greatly interested in physical science, and was also a patron of the liberal arts. His home was stored with the most beautiful products of the manufacturer's skill in fictile arts, and on its walls hung the most approved examples of the painter's skill. The looms of Holland and France and England furnished him with their delicate and sumptuous tapestries, and the Orient covered his floors with the richest and most prized carpets of Daghestan and Trebizond, and of Bokhara.

But even more marked than his love for art was his passion for physical science. His opportunities for the indulgence of this taste were unlimited, and the reinforcement of his natural aptitude by his great means enabled him to carry on experiments upon a scale of the most magnificent proportions. These experiments were made in a large building which was especially built for this object. It contained every facility for his various new designs, and in it he anticipated many advances in electrical science and in mechanical devices, which have made the civilization of our day so remarkable. I recall distinctly as a boy his ingenious approximation to the telephone, and even the recent advances in wireless telegraphy, which has been the instrumentality by which my own researches in the field of interplanetary telegraphy have been prosecuted, had been realized by himself.

It was in the midst of a life almost ideally happy that the blow fell which drove him and myself, then a boy and his only child, into a retirement which resulted in the discoveries I am about to relate. My father's devotion to my mother was an illustration of the most beautiful and tender love that a man can bear toward a woman. It was adoration. Though his mind was employed upon the abstruse questions of physics which he investigated, or edified by new acquisitions in art, all his knowledge and all his pleasure seemed but the means by which he endeavored to gain her deeper affection. She indeed became his companion in science, and her own just and well regulated taste constantly furnished him new motives for adding to his wide accumulations of art.

I can recall with some difficulty the day when with my father in a room immediately below the bedroom in which my mother was confined he awaited the summons of the doctors to see his wife for the last time. It was a rainy day, the clouds were drifting across a dull November sky. Through an opening in the trees then leafless, the Hudson was visible, even then flaked with ice, while an early snow covered the sloping lawn and whitened the broad-limbed oaks. I remember indistinctly his leading me by the hand through the hallway up the stairs, and softly whispering to me to be quite still, entered the large room dimly lit where my mother, attended by a nurse and a doctor, lay on the white bed. I remember being kissed by her and then being led from the room by the nurse. My father doubtless lingered until all was over, and the dear associate of his life, whose tenderness and charity had made all who approached her grateful, whose genial and appreciative mind had supplied the stimulus of recognition he needed for his own studies, passed away. After that I seemed dimly to recall a period of extreme loneliness when I was left in charge of a private instructor, while my father, as I later learned, bewildered by his great loss, and temporarily driven into a sort of madness, wandered in an aimless track of travel over the United States.

On his return the sharp recurrence to the scenes of his former happiness renewed the bitterness of his spirit, and he reluctantly concluded to abandon his home. His own thoughts had not as yet clearly formed any decision in his mind as to where he would go or what he would do. It was inevitable, however, that he should revert to his scientific investigations. He found in them a new solace and distraction, but even then his passion for research would not have sufficed to adequately meet his desperate desire to escape his grief, if in a rather singular manner there had not come to him an intimation of the possibilities of some sort of communication with my mother through these very investigations in electricity and magnetism in which he had been engaged.

I had become quite inseparable from him. He found in me many suggestions in face and manner of my mother, and particularly he was interested in my peculiar lapses into meditation and introspection which in many ways suggested to him a similar habit in her. On one occasion when, as was his wont, before we finally left the old home at Irvington, he had taken me in the summer evenings to the top of the observatory, then situated about half a mile west of the Albany road, we had both been silently watching the sun sink into a bank of golden haze, and the black band of the Palisades passing underneath like a velvet zone of shadow, I turned to my father and in a sudden access of curiosity said:

"Father, if mother had gone to the Sun, would she speak to us now with a ray of light?"

My father smiled patiently, half amused, and then standing and looking at the sun's disk, disappearing behind the Jersey hills, said, "My son, it was a curious thought of a well-known French writer, Figuer, who lost his son, who was very dear to him, that his soul with armies and hosts of other souls, had departed to the sun and that they made the light and heat of this great luminary, and this wise man felt some comfort in the thought that the heat and light of the sun as he felt himself bathed in radiance and warmth were emanations from his boy, and his eyes and body seemed then in a figurative, and yet to him, very real way, communicating with his boy. You smile. I know it is with interest. Let me read to you from Figuer's singular book what he has written about it."

He disappeared and left me also standing and looking upward at a faint wreath of cloud, tinged in rosiness, which floated almost in the zenith. I was then about eleven years old, precocious for my years and gifted with a sympathy for occult and difficult subjects that became only intensified through the peculiar concentrated companionship I had from day to day, and month to month enjoyed with my father.

This narrative may be inadvertently classed with those ephemeral fictions in which the reader is constantly conscious that the dialogue and the incidents are veritable creations. It may here be asked how could I recall with any literalness the conversations and events of a time so long past. I do not pretend or wish it to be thought that these interviews with my father are here literally related. That, of course, is beyond the limits of reasonable probability. But I do insist that in the following pages the occurrences described are very faithful transcripts of those connected with the peculiar inquiry and experiments my father and myself began, and brought to a startling conclusion. Although conducted in the form of an imaginative story the reader is importuned to give them his most implicit credence.

My father soon returned with the small volume of Figuer and read, I imagine, that passage which runs as follows in Chapter XIII:

"Since the sun is the first cause of life on our globe; since it is, as we have shown, the origin of life, of feeling, of thought; since it is the determining cause of all organized life on the earth—why may we not declare that the rays transmitted by the sun to the earth and the other planets are nothing more or less than the emanations of these souls? that these are the emissions of pure spirits living in the radiant star that come to us, and to dwellers in the other planets, under the visible form of rays?

"If this hypothesis be accepted, what magnificent, what sublime relations may we not catch a glimpse of, between the sun and the globes that roll around him; between the Sun and the planets there would be a continual exchange, a never broken circle, an unending 'come and go' of beamy emissions, which would engender and nourish in the solar world motion and activity, thought and feeling, and keep burning everywhere the torch of life.

"See the emanations of souls that dwell in the Sun descending upon the earth in the shape of solar rays. Light gives life to plants, and produces vegetable life, to which sensibility belongs. Plants having received from the Sun the germ of sensibility transmit it to animals, always with the help of the Sun's heat. See the soul germs enfolded in animals develop, improve little by little, from one animal to another, and at last become incarnated in a human body. See, a little later, the superhuman succeed the man, launch himself into the vast plains of ether, and begin the long series of transmigrations that will gradually lead him to the highest round of the ladder of spiritual growth, where all material substance has been eliminated, and where the time has come for the soul thus exalted, and with essence purified to the utmost, to enter the supreme home of bliss and intellectual and moral power; that is the Sun.

"Such would be the endless circle, the unbroken chain, that would bind together all the beings of Nature, and extend from the visible to the invisible world."

From that moment, moved more and more by the strangeness of the fancy, which evidently fascinated him, he buried himself in the indulgence of the thought of the possibility of some sort of communication with his wife. Singularly and fortunately he did not have recourse to the fruitless idiocy of spiritualism, nor engage in that humiliating intercourse with illiterate humbugs who personate the minds of men and women almost too sacred to be even for an instant associated in thought with themselves.

In 1881 electrical science had well advanced toward those perfected triumphs which give distinction to this century. Electric lighting was well understood, the Jablochkoff and Jamin lamps were then in use, the incandescent and Maxim light, or arc light were employed, and indeed the panic caused by Edison's premature announcement of the solution of the incandescent system of lighting had then preceded by two years, the excellent results of Mr. Swan in England in the same field. Edison's first carbon light and his original phonograph were exhibited toward the end of 1880 in the Patent Museum at South Kensington.

The daily News of New York in April of 1881 published the victory of the Edison Electric Lighting Company over the Mayor's veto in words that may be read to-day with considerable interest. It said "the company will proceed immediately to introduce its new electric lamps in the offices in the business portion of the city around Wall Street. It consists of a small bulbous glass globe, four inches long, and an inch and a half in diameter, with a carbon loop which becomes incandescent when the electric current passes through. Each lamp is of sixteen candle power with no perceptible variation in intensity. The light is turned on or off with a thumb screw. Wires have already been put into forty buildings."

My father had anticipated the incandescent light in its fuller later development and had used, before it was announced by Prof. Avenarius of Austria, a method of dividing the electric current, by the insertion of a polariser in a secondary circuit connected with each lamp, a method, it need not be said to electricians, now utterly obsolete.

The rooms of our physical laboratory at Irvington were almost all lit by electric lamps constructed somewhat on the principle of Edison's, but using platinum wires, and the old residents of that village may recall the singular, lonely house half hidden in broad sycamores, sending out its electric radiance late at night while my father and frequently myself, then a boy of thirteen years, worked at experimental problems in physics.

My father gave my precocity for science a very successful impetus and left me at his death fully in possession of the ideas and projects he cherished. Amongst these projects, one partially realized, was the acceleration of plant growth by means of electric light, and heating by electricity.

Dr. Siemens of England, it may be recalled, had very ingeniously experimented upon the influence of the electric light upon vegetation. In a paper read by that distinguished man before the Society of Telegraph Engineers in June, 1880, he referred to his conclusion that "electric light produces the coloring matter, chlorophyll, in the leaves of plants, that it aids their growth, counteracts the effects of night frosts, and promotes the setting and ripening of fruit in the open air."

I find in an old note book of my father's, dated 1879, "chlorophyllous matter in leaves encouraged by electric energy, presumably by the blue rays." In heating and cooking by electricity my father had made some progress though he had not in 1880 employed his time in this direction.

Perhaps more remarkable than anything else presenting my father's great scientific ingenuity was his improvements of the dynamo and the invention of a new successful small traction engine.

In 1880 the complete distinction between alternating and direct currents had not been made, and the device of a successful converter, for the change of the former comparatively inert to the latter's dynamic condition, only dreamed of. Yet in my father's notebook I find this suggestive sentence: "It seems possible to devise an apparatus which would deliver from an alternating circuit a direct current to a direct current circuit."

I have dwelt somewhat upon my father's scientific acquirements and genius in order to impress upon the reader the strictly legitimate training I received in scientific procedure, and I have instanced somewhat the status of his scientific development in 1880, because it was at that time that he concluded to leave Irvington and locate his laboratory and observatory elsewhere. And for the sake of his astronomical interests he determined to find some place peculiarly well fitted, on account of its atmospheric advantages, for astronomical observations. It is necessary likewise to recall some of the facts then known to astronomers and my father's own theories, in order to weave into a logical sequence the incidents leading up to my positive demonstration of a future life for some of our race in the planet Mars.

Astronomy had a great charm for my mother. Her enthusiasm was soon communicated to my father who found his wealth was a requisite in establishing the observatory he had erected at Irvington and in its equipment. Telescopes are expensive playthings.

The Lick Observatory was begun in 1880 and my father through correspondence with the directors of the University of California had learned many of the details pertaining to this great project. Influenced by the splendid prospects of this undertaking my father determined if possible to surpass it. He wrote to Fiel of Paris and expected to be able to secure an objective of 4 feet diameter, exceeding that of the Lick Observatory by one foot, a hopeless and as it proved an utterly abortive design. He spent an entire year in New York after leaving Irvington examining the various possible locations for his new observatory. The requisites were nearness to the equator, an equable climate, elevation and a clear atmosphere. During this year my father heard that Prof. Hertz of Berlin had generated waves of magnetism and that it was hoped that these might ultimately prove efficacious as a means of direct communication between distant points without the introduction of wire conductors.

This thought of communicating with distant points without fixed conductors greatly impressed my father and led him along a line of speculation upon which finally rested my own success in securing the messages detailed in this book from the planet Mars.

I recall that one evening in the winter of 1881 while he was yet engaged in making preparations for his departure from the United States to New Zealand, which he finally chose for the erection of his laboratories, and especially his observatory, I heard him read with the greatest satisfaction of the attempt made in the siege of Paris to bring the besieged French into telegraphic communication with the Provinces by means of the River Seine.

It was proposed to send powerful currents into the River Seine from batteries near the German lines and to receive in Paris upon delicate galvanometers, such an amount of their current as had not leaked away in the earth. Profs. Desains, Jamin, and Berthelot were interested in these experiments, although the suggestion had been made by M. Bourbouze, and after some interruptions when the attempt was to be carried out, the armistice of Jan. 14, 1871, brought their preparations to a close.

How often my father spoke of these attempts, and half smilingly on one occasion as we watched the starry skies "thick inlaid with patterns of bright gold" said to me: "It seems to me within the reach of possibility to attain some sort of connection with these shining hosts. If we must assume that the disturbances on the Sun's surface effect magnetic storms on ours, it is quite evident that a fluid of translatory power or consistency exists between the earth and the sun, then also between all the planetary inhabitants of space, and I cannot see why we may not hope some day to realize a means of communication with these distant bodies. How inspiring is the thought that in some such way upon the basis of an absolutely perfect scientific deduction we might be brought into conversational alliance with these singular and orderly creations, and actually look upon their scenes and lives and history, and bring to ourselves in verbal pictures a presentation of their marvellous properties."

I think it was on this occasion that my father expressed his thought upon some form of interplanetary telegraphy in a manner that left it in my own mind a very impressive and majestic idea. He had read at some length the address of Sir William Armstrong before the British Association in 1863, when that distinguished observer speaks of the sympathy between forces operating in the sun, and magnetic forces in the earth and remarks the phenomenon seen by independent observers in September, 1859. The passage, easily verified by the reader, was to this effect:

"A sudden outburst of light, far exceeding the brightness of the sun's surface was seen to take place, and sweep like a drifting cloud over a portion of the solar surface. This was attended by magnetic disturbances of unusual intensity and with exhibitions of aurora of extraordinary brilliancy. The identical instant at which the effusion of light was observed was recorded by an abrupt and strongly marked deflection in the self-registering instruments at Kew."

My father then pausing and walking impetuously across the room declaimed, as it were, his views:

"Here we are, a group of limited intelligent beings circumscribed by a boundless space, and placed upon a speck of matter which is whirled around the sun in an endless captivity, bound by this inexorable law of gravitation, like a stone in a sling. About us in this ethereal ocean floats a host of similarly made orbs, perhaps, in thousands of cases, inhabited by beings throbbing with the same curiosity as our own to reach out beyond their sphere, and learn something of the nature of the animated universe which they may dimly suspect lies about them in the other stars. Why must it not be part of this immeasurable design which brought us here, that we shall some day become part of a celestial symposium; that lines of communication, invisible but incessant, shall thread in labyrinths of invisible currents these dark abysses, and bring us in inspiring touch with the marvels and contents of the entire universe."

He turned to me and gazing intently at my upturned face which I am sure reflected his own in its enthusiasm and delight, continued: "You, my son, and I, will put this before us as a possible achievement and work incessantly for that end. Prof. Hertz has generated these magnetic waves; we will; and by means of some sort of a receiver endeavor to find out a clue to *wireless telegraphy*." These closing remarkable words were actually used by my father, and in view of the marvellous realization of Marconi's hopes in that direction, as well as my own stupendous success in reaching the inhabitants of Mars, was a distinct prophecy.

It was a few months later that my father completed all of his arrangements in regard to the disposition of his investments, and perfected the necessary arrangements for being constantly supplied with funds by his bankers in New York. He also had agreed upon the apparatus to be forwarded, expecting to be largely supplied at Sydney in new South Wales, as it was from this point he intended to sail or steam to New Zealand. Much of the equipment for his observatory was to come from Paris, and he relied upon intelligent assistance both in Sydney and Christ Church, in New Zealand, for the erection and furnishment of his various houses.

He finally concluded to place his station on Mount Cook at an elevation of 1,000 feet upon a well protected plateau, which was described to him by a Mr. Ashton who had extensive acquaintance and some five years' experience in New Zealand. We found this position ideal, and in the perfection of all the conditions necessary for our experiments possessed by it, made the realization at that time utterly unsuspected by either of us, of our final designs, commensurately more simple.

I left New York with my father filled with a curious expectancy. I seemed to cherish no regret at leaving my childhood's home. I only felt a vague wondering delight to go abroad and see strange and new things. My seclusion with my father had developed in me a singular inaptitude for companionship with boys of my own age, and furthermore from the influence of his rather poetic and dreaming nature, I began to show a half wistful intensity of interest in things occult, mysterious and difficult. We left New York in 1882, and it was then that I read for diversion in my long ride to California, Colonel Olcutt's Esoteric Buddhism.

The whole central fancy of reincarnation affected me deeply. But I modified the idea as displayed by Blavatsky and Theosophists generally. From a long familiarity with the stars, in conjunction with the inevitable creative and anthropomorphic sensibility of youth, I began to think that this reincarnation did not occur on the earth, but had its stages of transmutation placed elsewhere. In short, I amused myself incessantly with placing the poets in one star, the novelists in another, the scientists in a third, the mechanicians in a fourth, and in each I imagined a Utopia. A very little mature thought and the most ordinary observation of plain men, men who at 20 have far more practical sense than I possess to-day, would have demonstrated the hopelessness of this arrangement, and the deplorable social chaos it would have led to.

I think, however, that along this line of feeling I grew more and more in sympathy with my father's dimly expressed hopes to achieve something tangible in the way of interstellar or planetary communication. So that gradually he, by reason of a desire that slowly invaded every emotional recess of his being, and I, through the vagaries of an imaginative mind reached successively an intense conviction that we should work in this direction.

There was much in our scientific work also that encouraged a certain high mindedness and liberty of speculation, a careless audacity before the most difficult tasks. The resolution of matter into a phase of energy, the interpretation of light as an electric phenomenon, the mysteries of the electric force itself, the peculiar hypotheses about the force of gravitation, lead men, studying these subjects, and endowed with speculative tendencies to conceive, moved also by a quasi sensational desire to reach new results, that the most extravagant achievements are possible to science.

With us, regarding the physical universe as a unit, recognizing the notes of intelligence of a deep coercive and comprehensive plan involved throughout, feeling that our human intelligence was the reflex or microcosmic representation of the planning, upholding mind, that if so, no conceivable limitation could be placed upon its expansion and conquests, that further it would be incomprehensible that the colonizing (so to speak) of the central mind occurred only on one sphere, when it doubtless might be embodied in other beings, on hundreds or thousands or millions of other spheres; that continuance of life after death was a truth; feeling all this, their concomitant influence was to make us positive that the human mind in an intelligent, satisfactory, self-illuminating way some day would reach mind everywhere in all its specific forms; and that the abyss of space would eventually thrill with the vibrations of conscious communion between remote worlds.

With feelings of this sort excited and reinforced by my father's passionate hope to learn something of his wife's life after death we reached Christ Church, New Zealand, in June, 1883.

I may now revert to the line of suggestions that led my father and myself to locate in Mars the scene, at least, as we surmised in part, of those phases of a future life which I am now able to reveal with, I think, positive certainty.

The planet Mars as being the next orb removed from the Sun after our own world in the advance outward from our solar center, has always attracted attention. At perihelion, when in opposition with the earth, it is 35 millions of miles from the earth, and its surface, as is well known from the drawings of Kaiser, the Leyden astronomer, and of Schiaparelli, Denning, Perrotin and Terby, has apparently revealed an alternation of land and water which, with the assumption of meteorological conditions, such as prevail on the earth, has gradually made it easy to think of its occupation by rational beings as altogether possible.

During the opposition of Mars in 1879-80, Prof. Schiaparelli at Milan determined for the second time the topography of this planet. The topography revealed the curious long lines or ribbons, commonly called canals, which seamed the face of our neighboring planet. In 1882 this observation was enormously extended. He then showed that there was a variable brightness in some regions, that there had been a progressive enlargement since 1879 of his *Syrtis Magna*, that the oblique white streaks previously seen, continued, and, more remarkable, that there was a continuous development day after day of the doubling of the canals which seemed to extend along great circles of the sphere. In 1882 Schiaparelli expected at the evening opposition in 1884 to confirm and add to these observations.

My father had read Schiaparelli's announcements with absorbed interest. They fed his burning fancies as to the extension of our present life, and offered him a sort of scientific basis (without which he was inclined to view all eschatology as superficial) for the belief that we may attain in some other planet an actual prolonged second existence.

His great reverence for Sir William Herschell was indisputable. He quoted Herschell's own words with appreciation. These pregnant sentences were as follows:

"The analogy between Mars and the earth is perhaps by far the greatest in the whole solar system. Their diurnal motion is nearly the same, the obliquity of their respective ecliptics not very different; of all the superior planets the distance of Mars from the sun is by far the nearest, alike to that of the earth; nor will the length of the Martial year appear very different from what we enjoy when compared to the surprising duration of the years of Jupiter, Saturn and the Georgian Sidus. If we then find that the globe we inhabit has its polar region frozen and covered with mountains of ice and snow, that only partially melt when alternately exposed to the sun, I may well be permitted to surmise that the same causes may probably have the same effect on the globe of Mars; that the bright polar spots are owing to the vivid reflection of light from frozen regions; and that the reduction of these spots is to be ascribed to their being exposed to the sun."

"In the light of these larger analogies," my father would continue, "why are we not further permitted to conclude that there is a more intimate and minute correlation. Why can not we predicate that under similar climatic and atmospheric vicissitudes, with a very probably similar or identical origin with our globe, this planet Mars, now burning red in the evening skies, possesses life, an organic retinue of forms like our own, or at least involving such primary principles as respiration, assimilation and productiveness, as would produce some biological aspects not extremely differing from those seen in our own sphere.

"If we imagine, as we are most rationally allowed to, that Mars has undergone a progressive secularization in cooling, that contraction has acted upon its surface as it has on ours, that water has accumulated in basins and depressed troughs, that atmospheric currents have been started, that meteorological changes in consequence have followed, and that the range of physical conditions embraces phases naturally very much like those that have prevailed in our planet, how can it be intelligently questioned that from these very identical circumstances, an order of life has not in some way arisen."

My father had an interesting habit of snapping his fingers on both hands together over his head when he declaimed in this way, always circling about the room in a rapid stride. I remember he stopped in front of me and continued in a strain something like this:

"For myself I am convinced that there has been an evolution in the order of beings from one planet to another, that there is going on a stream of transference, from one plane of life here to planes elsewhere, and that the stream is pouring in as well as out of this world, and that it may be, in our case, pouring both ways, that is, we may be losing individuals into lower grades of life as well as emitting them to higher. See, what economy!

"Instead of wasting the energies of imagination to account for the destinations of millions upon millions of human beings, the countless host that has occupied the surfaces of this earth through all the historic and prehistoric ages, we can, upon this assumption, reduce the number of individuals immensely, allowing that spirits are constantly arriving, constantly departing, and that the sum total in the solar system remains perhaps nearly fixed, just as in the electrolysis of water we have hydrogen rising at one electrode and oxygen at the other by transmission of atoms of hydrogen and atoms of oxygen toward each electrode through the water itself, in opposite directions, while for a sensible time the mass of water remains unchanged.

"Let us suppose that in Mercury some form of mental life exists, that it is individualized, that it expresses the physical constants of that globe, that its mentality has reached the point where it can make use of the resources of Mercury, can respond to its physical constants so far as they awaken poetry or art or religion or science. Suppose that this life is one of extreme forcefulness, of stress and storm, like some prehistoric condition on our globe, but invested with more intellectual attributes than the same ages on our earth required or possessed, perhaps reaching a permanent condition not unlike that depicted in the Niebelungen Lied or the Sagas of the North. It might be called the *brawn* period. Then the spirits born upon our planet or on any other planet in an identical condition, would find after death their destination in Mercury, where they could evolve up to the point where they might return to as, or to some other planet fitted for a higher life.

"Then Venus, we may imagine, succeeding Mercury, carries a higher type, an emotional life, though of course I am not influenced by her accidental name, in suggesting it. Here in Venus, a period perchance resembling a mixture of the pagan Grecian life and the troubadour life of

Provence may prevail and again to it have flown the spirits which in our planet only touch that development, which from Venus flow to us, those adapted for the religious or intellectual phase we present. This Venus life might be called the *sense* period.

"And now our world follows, with its scientific life which probably represents its normal limit. Beyond this it will not go. As we have developed through a *brawn* and *sense* period to our present stage, so in Mercury and Venus, ages have prevailed of development which eventuated in their final fixed stages at brawn and sense. In Venus, too, the brawn stage preceded the sense period. In us both have preceded the scientific stage. There has been, may we not think, constant interchanges between these planets of such lives as survive material dissolution, and they have found the *nidus* that fits them in each. Souls leaving us in a brawn *epoch* have fled to Mercury, souls leaving us in a *sense* epoch have fled to Venus, and all souls in Mercury or Venus, ready for reincarnation in a *scientific* epoch, have come to us.

"But there is an important postulate underlying this theory. It is, that upon each planet the possibilities of development just attain to the margin of the next higher step in mental evolution. That is, that on Mercury the period of brawn develops to the possibility of the period of sense without fully exemplifying it, so in Venus the period of sense develops to the possibility of the period of science without attaining it, and in our world the period of science develops to the period of *spirit*, without, in any universal way, exhibiting it.

"These are steps progressively represented, I may imagine, in the planets. And, in the further progress outward, we reach the planet Mars. Let us place here the period of spirit. On Mars is accomplished in society, and accompanied by an accomplishment in its physical features, also, of those ideals of living which the great and good unceasingly labor to secure for us here and unceasingly fail to secure. O my child, if we could learn somehow to get tidings from that distant sphere, if only the viewless abyss of space between our world and Mars might be bridged by the *noiseless and unseen waves of a magnetic current*."

We reached Christ Church in June, in 1883, and for one year were most busy in completing the station we had selected, in receiving apparatus, getting our observatory built and a useful, but not large telescope mounted.

The position taken by us was attractive. It was upon a high hill, a glacial mound which had been smoothed upon its upper surface into a long and broad plain. The prospects from this position were exceedingly beautiful. Christ Church was some ten miles distant and the irregular shores northward outlined by ribbons of breaking waves lay upon the seaward margin of our vision, while the broken intermediate landscape, with interrupted agricultural domains and forests was in front of us and far above us rose the grander peaks of the New Zealand Alps, a constant charm through the changing atmosphere, now brought near to us through the optical refraction of the clear air, and again veiled and shadowed and removed into spectral evanescent forms. The picture was intensely interesting and like all commanding views where the most expressive elements of scenery are combined, the remote sea, reflecting every mood of light and color, and the snowy peaks carrying to us the opaline glories of rising or setting sun was a comparison that stimulated and controlled the spectator with its wonderful charm and strength and poetic changes.

To me whose emotional nature, inherited from a mother gifted with delicate tastes and a refined enthusiasm for the beautiful had been curiously discouraged by association with my father's scientific pursuits, this lively panorama constantly fed my dreams with pleasing pictures.

My life has been an isolated and repressed one, except for the one incident I am about to bequeath to posterity. I had not enjoyed the play of youthful companions except in a fugitive way, I had not gone to school nor passed three years of muscular and buoyant activity in the usual pastimes and pleasures of childhood. I had a precocious nature and it had been unfolded in an atmosphere of strictly intellectual ideas. My mother had been a constant joy to me during the short years of her life on earth, but somehow by reason of sickness I had not enjoyed even her endearment as I might have.

So in my father and his aspirations, and the later hopes of his excited and passionate longing to regain some trace of my mother, my life from four years of age was actually and potentially concentrated. My father cherished me with a great consuming love. He saw in me the representation in face and partially in temperament of his wife. He lavished on me every care. Yet because of his eager affection, and his complete suspense from social connections I was made too largely dependent on him alone. I lived in his companionship only. My conversation became prematurely advanced in terms and principles, and my childish confidence was nurtured by nothing less wonderful than books and theories, experiments and dissertations.

The wonderful beauty of our new surroundings, the strangeness of our sudden removal from America, the long distances travelled, awoke in me new thoughts and I readily surrendered myself at times to the incoherent struggles of my nature, to find someone, something, more responsive to my young feelings than essays on magnetism, and a man, father though he was, immersed in demonstrations and problems. It was then that this distant picture in the days of the fragrant and reviving springtime, filled me with unutterable and touching ecstacy.

My father, as I had said, fully intended to arrive at some definite conclusions as to the possibilities of wireless telegraphy. At one end of the grassy plain I have alluded to, our chief stations were erected and, at the distance of two miles, almost at the other extremity, we placed a smaller station. Our whole work was to achieve telegraphic communication between these points without wires. At night my father bent his telescopic gaze upon the heavens, and as the earth approached opposition to Mars in 1884 I remember his eagerness and his repeated adjurations that if we failed in the task in his lifetime I should devote my life, separated from all other occupations and indulgences, to carrying on his designs.

At first he only dimly intimated his great ambition, the union of our world with others by magnetic waves, but as it slowly assumed a theoretical certainty he talked more and more boldly of this portentous and transforming possibility.

I cannot refrain from noticing another important scientific activity of my father's. It was the use of photography in stellar measurement. As is well known to photographers, in 1871 Dr. R.L. Maddox used gelatine in place of collodion from which innovation rose the present system of dry plate photography. My father had always felt the greatest interest in the use of photography in astronomy. He was acquainted with the splendid work done by Chapman for Rutherford, New York, in his careful and exquisite photographs of the moon. As early as 1850 Whipple of Boston made photographs of the stars.

It was, however, the incomparable advantages, furnished in speed, by the dry plate photography which made my father realize early as anyone, the boundless possibilities thus opened in human attainment for the penetration of the Sidereal firmament. He had made a great number of photographs at Irvington, and the photographic laboratory was a charming illustration of my father's ingenuity and precision. At Mt. Cook we enjoyed a marvellously clear atmosphere for work of this sort, and amongst the first thoughts of my father was to provide the most satisfactory means for the continuance of our stellar photography. Besides our visual telescope we had a photographic telescope which was used, instead of connecting the visual lens on one and the same instrument, as in the Lick Observatory.

The innovations introduced by photography have revolutionized the processes of stellar measurement. Instead of the laborious task of measuring the stars through the telescope, the photographic plate can be studied at ease as a correct and identical chart of the heavens and the results thus obtained placed at the disposal of astronomers. My father appreciated this and amongst his numerous projects of scientific usefulness the preparation of photographs of the stars fully occupied his mind.

We had no Meridian Circle, as it was less in the direction of the determination of the position of stars than in the elucidation of the surfaces of planets, that my father's astronomical predilections lay. Our telescope was a refractor and had an objective of two feet diameter. It was firmly supported on a trap rock pedestal. The eye piece adjustment was unusually successful, and the remarkable freedom of the objective from any traces of spherical or chromatic aberration gave us an image of surprising clearness. The photographic results were admirable. I imagine few more satisfactory photographs of the face of Moon have been made than those we secured, so far at least as definition is concerned, and the detail within the limits of our powers of magnification.

The telescope was very slowly installed and it was well in 1885 before we were able to use it for either observation or photography.

As the surprising messages detailed in the following pages came by means of wireless telegraphy, I will dwell for an instant for the benefit of the non-scientific reader, upon the investigations made by my father and myself in this subject.

The installation of a wireless telegraphic station is not necessarily difficult. The progress made since my father and myself began these experiments has been, of course, considerable, and yet so far as I am able to ascertain the new devices in this direction were largely anticipated by us. The tuning of wireless messages by which the interception of messages is prevented was certainly forestalled by us, though in the communications with Mars herein detailed the ordinary [*non-syntonic.*—Editor] receiver was employed.

We employed an induction coil, emitted a wave by a spark, and had a wire rod [*antenna.*—Editor] which was in turn part of an induction coil. This was the sender (transmitter) and we could regulate the wave length so that a receiving wire adjusted for such a wave could only receive it. [There seems to be implied in these words an arrangement known as the Slaby-Arco system, which American readers have had described for them by M.A. Frederick, Collins, Sci. Amer., March 9 and Dec. 28, 1901.—Editor.] The receiver consisted of iron filings in which later carbon particles were added.

My father died in 1892 and we had not at the time of his death learned of Popoff's microphone-coherer in which steel filings were mixed with carbon granules. The magnetic waves received at first by us presumably from Mars, and later, as the communications indisputably show, from that planet, were taken upon a Marconi receiver, or what was practically that.

My father became more and more interested in the direction of interplanetary research by means of the magnetic wave. He argued vehemently, buoyed up by his increasingly augmented hopes as our own experiments improved, that the electric wave through space moving in an ethereal fluid of the extremest purity would progress more rapidly than in our atmosphere, that the tension of such waves would be greater, that they could be so "heaped up" as he expressed it—(*In the Slaby-Arco system an apparatus is employed consisting of a Ruhmkorff coil with a centrifugal mercury interrupter, by which a steeper wave front of the disruptive discharge is secured.—* Editor)—that their reception over the almost impassable distances of space would be made possible.

This idea of piling up the waves was suggested by purely physical analogies. The enormous waves generated by severe storms upon the ocean travel farther than the smaller waves, and are less consecutively dissipated by the resistance of the water, the traction of its molecules and the occasional diversion of cross disturbances from other centers.

Again some experiments made invacuo upon a limited scale seemed to show the accuracy of his predictions. Through a glass tube one foot in diameter and ten feet long we sent magnetic waves both when the tube was filled with air and when it was exhausted. Our means of measuring the time required in both cases were quite inadequate—perhaps there was no appreciable difference—but the records in the latter case, secured upon a Morse register, were unmistakably more vigorous and audible.

At last our various results had reached a point where we felt justified in extending the limits of our investigations. We had up to this time only tried our messages between the two stations upon the plateau of Mt. Cook. My father now proposed that I go to Christ Church, install a sender (transmitter) and send messages to him at the observatory. I did so and the experiment was convincing. The day before I was ready to transmit a message I had attended an attractive church service—it was toward the close of Lent in the year 1889—and as my father was entirely unprepared for the account I proposed to give him of the function, I thought its correct transmission would afford an indubitable proof of our success. I wrote out the description. It was received by my father with only ten imperfect interpretations in a list of 1,000 words.

From this time forward our plans for erecting a receiver in the observatory were pushed to a completion. We had discovered the necessity of elevation for the senders (transmitters) and receivers for long distance work, and a tall mast, fifty feet in height, was put up at the observatory, which—needlessly I think—was to serve as the terrestrial station for the reception of those viewless waves which my father thought might be constantly breaking unrecorded upon the insensitive surfaces of our earth.

The eventful night came. It was August, 1890. Mars was then in opposition. The evening had been extremely beautiful. Nature united in her mood the most transporting contradictions of temperament. It was August and the day had been marked by changes of almost tropical severity, although, as we were south of the equator (the latitude of Christ Church is S. 44 degrees) August was, with us, mid-winter. A thunderstorm had broken upon us in the morning, itself an unusual meteorological phenomenon, and the downpour of black rain, shutting off the views and enclosing us in a torrential embrace of floods, had lasted an hour when it passed away, and the Sun re-illumined the wide glistening scene. The line of foam from the breakers along the remote shore, yet lashing with curbing crests the inlets, promontories, and islands, was readily seen; the northern Alps shone in their ermine robes, greatly lengthened and deepened by the season's snows, the washed country side below us was a patch work of rocks and fields and denuded forestland. Christ Church like a vision of whiteness sprang out to the west upon our vision, and immediately about us the mingling rivulets poured their musical streams through and over the icy banks of half consolidated snow.

As night came up, the stars seemed almost to pop out in their appropriate places, like those stellar illusions that appear so appropriately upon the theatrical stage, and the low lying moon sent its flickering radiance over the yet unsubdued waters. It was the time of the opposition of Mars which brings that planet nearest to us. As is well known to astronomers, the perihelion of Mars is in the same longitude in which the earth is on August 27; and when an opposition occurs near that date, the planet is only 35 millions of miles from the earth, and this is the closest approach which their bodies can ever make.

Our magnetic receiver had been placed in position, the Morse register was attached; the whole apparatus was in one of the upper rooms of the observatory, in proximity with the telescope through whose glass for days we had watched the approach of our sister planet. As the night settled down upon us we had taken our seats for a few instants at a table in a lower room engaged in one of those innumerable desultory talks upon our project and their, even to us, somewhat problematic character. Everything connected with that evening, apart from its having been carefully recorded in my diary and notebooks, is very distinctly remembered by me. I recall my father reading from a letter to Nature, May 15, 1884, by Mr. W.F. Denning, discussing "The Rotation Period of Mars." From my note-book I find the passage literally transcribed:

It read—"Notwithstanding his comparatively small diameter and its slow axial motion, the planet Mars affords especial facilities for the exact determination of the rotation period. Indeed, no other planet appears to be so favorably circumstanced in this respect, for the chief markings on Mars have been perceptible with the same definiteness of outline and characteristics of form through many succeeding generations, whereas the features, such as we discern on the other planets, are either temporary, atmospheric phenomena, or rendered so indistinct by unfavorable conditions as to defy measurement and observation. Moreover, it may be taken for granted that the features of Mars are permanent objects on the actual surface of the planet, whereas the markings displayed by our telescopes on some of the other planetary members of our system are mere effects of atmospheric changes, which, though visible for several years and showing well defined periods of rotation cannot be accepted as affording the true periods. The behavior of the red spot on Jupiter may closely intimate the actual motion of the sphere of that planet, but markings of such variable, unstable character can hardly exhibit an exact conformity of motion with the surface upon which they are seen to be projected. With respect to Mars' case, it is entirely different. No substantial changes in the most conspicuous features have been detected since they were first confronted with telescopic power and we do not anticipate that there will be any material difference in their general configurations.

"The same markings which were indistinctly revealed to the eyes of Fontana and Huyghens in 1636 and 1659 will continue to be displayed to the astronomers of succeeding generations, though with greater fullness and perspicuity owing to improved means. True, there may possibly be variations in progress as regards some of the minor features, for it has been suggested that the visibility of certain spots has varied in a manner which cannot be satisfactorily accounted for on ordinary grounds. These may possibly be due to atmospheric effects on the planet itself, but in many cases the alleged variations have doubtless been more imaginary than real. The changes in our own climate are so rapid and striking, and occasion such abnormal appearances in celestial objects that we are frequently led to infer actual changes where none have taken place; in fact, observers cannot be too careful to consider the origin of such differences and to look nearer home for some of the discordances which may have become apparent in their results."

It was just as he finished reading this extract that the shrill fluttering call of the maxy bird was heard from the bare branches of a poplar near the station, and in the next instant, in that intense quiet that succeeds sometimes a sudden unexpected and acute accent, the Morse register was audible above us, clicking with a continuity and evident *intention* that, weighted as we were with vague sensational hopes, drew the blood from our faces, and seemed almost like a voice from the red orb then glowing in the southeastern sky. We sprang together up the stairs to the operating-room and saw with our eyes the moving lever of the little Morse machine. We had made ourselves familiar with the ordinary telegraphic codes, the international Telegraphic Code and that in use in Canada and the United States. They were useless. The succession of short or long intervals was entirely different and the message, if message it was, defied our persistent efforts at translation. The disturbance of the register continued some three hours, and though we were unmistakably in communication with some external regulated and *intentional* source of magnetic impulses we were hopelessly confused as to their meaning.

I can never forget our excitement. We were certainly the recipient of exact careful conscious messages. Their terrestrial origin, strange and incredible as it might appear, did not seem likely, for the two codes so generally in use were not represented in it. Could it be—the thought seemed to stop the beating of our hearts—could it be that we had indeed received an extra-terrestrial communication? The register of the dots and dashes cannot be all reproduced here, though a very long record of them, indeed almost complete, was made by myself. During the whole time that the register moved hardly a word of conversation escaped our lips. We were fixed in mute amazement. We were full of unexpressed imaginings, which were told, however in my father's face, so flushed with eagerness, as with half-parted lips he bent over the instrument or interrupted his attention by walking to the window and gazing far out into the heavens.

The record we obtained is here reproduced, in part, as the whole would occupy altogether too much space. I am interested in giving it as it may effectually remain a proof of my sincerity in this matter, and will, I have the firm conviction, be repeated in the future, not exactly or at all, as I have written it, but some message similarly received will corroborate the statement here made, and the still further marvellous facts I am yet to relate.

The record I will select for reproduction is as follows:

```
... - ...— ... - - . - . - ... - . - - - - - - ... - - - .......- - .. . . . . - - - . . . . . -
- - - - - - - - - - - - . , . . - - . , . . . - - - - - . . . . . . . - - - . . - . . . - - - - - . . . . . . . . -
- . - . . . . . - - . . , - - - - - - - - - - - - - - . . . . . . . . . . - - - - - - - - - - - -
- - - - - - . . . . - . . . . - - - . . . - . . . . - . . . - - - - . . . . - - - . . . . . . -
```

CHAPTER II

As I now know there is a Martian language, if this communication came from that planet, which was my own and my father's deepest conviction, it would be impossible to interpret the foregoing record with any certainty, or indeed, in any way. Absolute ignorance of that language, except the brief mention in my father's communications, received by myself from that body—whose publication before I die is the sole purpose of this manuscript—make it quite certain that it is in the main a vowel language, consisting of short vocalic syllables. In such a case it is probable that some abbreviation has been used, and the problem of its resolution simply is placed out of the question. I may here partially forestall the facts communicated to me by my father from Mars. In those unparalleled messages he has told me of the desire of the Martians to communicate with the earth, and as the Martians themselves are largely made up of transplanted human spirits, the possibility of doing so would have been completely expected. But the singular evanescence of memory amongst these humans which absolutely displaces details of strictly mnemonic acquirements, except in certain directions of art and invention, has apparently precluded this.

We remained at the register almost the entire night taking turns in our tireless vigil. But no more disturbances occurred. My father was deeply moved and I scarcely less so. Accustomed as we had become to the thought that wireless telegraphy would place us more readily in touch with the sidereal universe than with distant points upon our earth, presuming indeed, that, except for the intervening envelopes of atmosphere attached to our or any neighboring planet, the path of transmission of messages through space would be inconceivably swift, we saw nothing really impossible in the impression that we had that night received communications from extra-terrestrial sources.

The thought was none the less stupendous, and it seemed almost impossible for us to allude to the subject without a peculiar sense of reverential self-suppression, at least for a week or so. Examination and inquiry showed us no contiguous source of the message and it seemed most improbable that it had come to us from any distant part of the earth, as we had become acquainted with the difficulty or impossibility of bridging our very great distances with the resources then at human command, and with the unavoidable exigence of the earth's convexity.

* * * * *

It was a few months after this that my father, returning from a climb in the neighboring hills, complained of great weariness and a sort of mild vertigo. I had become exceedingly endeared to him. I found him a most unusual companion, and unnaturally separated as I had been from more ordinary associations, our lives had assumed an almost fraternal tenderness.

I was greatly troubled to see my father's illness, and begged him to take rest; indeed, to leave the observatory for a while; to visit Christ Church. We had made some very congenial acquaintances in Christ Church. A family of Tontines and a gentleman and his daughter by the name of Dodan had often visited us, and while we had become somewhat a subject of perennial curiosity, and were more or less visited by curiosity hunters and others, actuated by more intelligent motives, the Tontines and the Dodans remained our only very intimate friends.

Indeed, Miss Dodan had come to me, buried in scientific speculations and denied hitherto all female acquaintants, like a beam of light through a sky not at all dark, but gray and pensive and sometimes almost irksome. Miss Katharine Dodan was gentle, pretty, and unaffectedly enthusiastic. Her interest in all equipment of our laboratories was boundless. When I found myself alone with her at the big telescope adjusting everything with—oh! such exquisite precision—and then sometimes discovered my hand resting upon hers, or my head touching those silken brown curves of hair that framed her white brow and reddening cheeks, the throbbing pleasure was so sweet, so unexpected, so strange, that I felt a new desire rise in my heart, and the newness of life lifted me for a moment out of myself, and started those fires of ambition and hope that only a lovely woman can awaken in the heart of a man. I mention this circumstance that led to the fatal train of occurrences that led to my father's death.

I urged my father to go to Christ Church and stay with the Dodans. Mr. Dodan had frequently invited him, and Miss Dodan's brightness and her cheerful art at the piano would, I know, cheer him, inured too long to his lonely life, subject to the periodic returns of that bitter sadness, which was now only accentuated by his self-imposed exile from the home and scenes of his former happiness.

He at last consented, and in October, 1891, accompanied by the Dodans, whom he had summoned from Christ Church, he went down the steep hillside that slanted from our plateau to the lowlands, and was soon lost from view in a turn of the road, which also robbed me of the sight of a waving, small white handkerchief, floating in front of a half-loosened pile of chestnut hair.

A few days later I received a visit from Miss Dodan. I was then working at some photographs in the dark room. My assistant told me of her arrival.

I hurried to our little reception room and library, where a few of my father's "Worthies of Science" decorated the walls, which for the most part were covered with irregular book cases, while a long square covered table occupied the center of the room, littered with charts, maps, journals and daily papers.

Miss Dodan sat near the wide window looking toward Christ Church and the quickly descending road over which only a few days ago my father had journeyed. I caught in her face, as I entered, an anxious and disturbed glance, and I felt almost instantly an intimation of disaster. She turned to me as I came into the room and with a quick movement advanced.

"Mr. Dodd, your father is ill. I hardly know what is the matter with him. He is quite strange; does not know us when we talk to him, and wanders in a talk about 'magnetic waves' and 'his wife' and 'different code.' Won't you come to see him? You may help him greatly."

The kind, clear eyes looked up into mine and the impulse of real sympathy as she pressed my hand seemed unmistakable. I asked a few questions and was convinced that my father was the victim of some sort of shock, perhaps precipitated by the continuous excitement caused by our unaccountable experience in the observatory.

I was but a few moments getting ready for the drive to Christ Church. I remember the cold, crisp air, the rapid motion, and can I ever forget it—the nearness and touch of Miss Dodan's person, perhaps only a hurried brushing past me of her arm, the stray touch of her floating hair, or the accidental stubbing of her foot against my own. It seemed a short, delicious drive. I fear my heart was almost equally divided between apprehension for my father's health and the joy of simple nearness to the woman I loved. At last we reached Christ Church. The Dodans lived in the suburbs in a pretty villa on a high hill, from whose top the city lay spread before them in its modest extent with its neighboring places and Port Lyttelon eight miles away.

I found my father better, but it required my own zeal and affection to thoroughly restore him, and bring him back to his characteristic interest and alertness, which made him so original and delightful a companion. At length, by a week's nursing, during which Miss Dodan and myself were frequently together, becoming more and more attached to each other, my father renewed his wonted studies, and strongly desired to return to the "plateau."

I almost regretted, harsh as the thought may seem, our return. Such incidents are now a kind of sweet sadness to recall, for as I write these words, I hear nearer and nearer the summons that must put me also in the spirit world, while she, in whose heart my own trustingly lived, has been taken away, I think wisely and prudently, to live with her father's people in a charming, rustic village of Devonshire. But oh! so far away! and this picture which daily I draw from beneath the pillow of my sick couch must alone serve to replace the companionship of her face and voice.

I can permit myself in this last record of an unrecoverable past to describe a treasured incident just before I left the Dodan home with my father. I was coming out of my room when I found Miss Dodan also emerging from her own bedroom at the opposite end of an upper hall. We met and I said: "Miss Dodan, it is a treacherous confession, but I wish you were going back with us, or that my father would stay a little longer here. I shall miss you."

"Yes," she answered. "Aren't you a good nurse?"

"Oh, I think you need not misunderstand me," I insisted.

"Misunderstanding is rather an English trait, you Americans say," she retorted.

"But in this case," I continued, "I hoped any disadvantages of that sort would be overcome by your own feelings."

She blushed and looked quite dauntlessly into my eyes: "You mean," she inquired, "that you are sorry to leave me?"

My face was very red, I knew, and I felt a puzzling sensation in my throat, but I did not hesitate: "Of course, I am sorry to leave you, more sorry than I can say, but I fear more, that leaving you may mean losing you."

This time confusion seemed struggling with a pleased mirth in her face, and with a laugh and a quick movement toward the stairway she exclaimed: "Well, Americans, they say, never lose what they really care to win."

I darted forward, but she was too quick for me and the chase ended in the lower hall in a group of people—her parents, my father, visitors and servants—and I saw her disappear with a backward glance, in which, I could swear, I saw two pouting lips.

My father was overjoyed to return to our really very comfortable quarters on "Martian Hill," as Mr. Dodan, in reference to my father's infatuation over his imaginary (?) population of Mars, was accustomed to call our professional home.

It was, I think, only a few weeks after this that my father called me to his room. He was standing in his morning apparel, a strange garb which he sometimes affected, made up of a black velvet gown brought together at the waist by a stout yellow cord, a bright red skull cap, a sort of sandal shoe, picked out with silver ornaments, his arms covered with loose, puckered sleeves of lace, dotted with black extending up to the close fitting sleeves of the velvet gown which only descended to his elbow. Beneath the gown, when he was thus theatrically attired, he wore a shirt of pale blue silk with a flat collar, over which came a black vest meeting his black trunks and blue hose.

My father was a really striking and beautiful picture in his incongruous habiliment. His strong and thoughtful face, over which yet clustered the curly hair of boyhood, just touched with gray, lit up by his earnest, sad eyes, seemed—how distinctly I recall it—almost ideally lovely that morning, and I compared him in my thoughts with the father of Romola, only as wearing a more youthful expression. He was seated when I came in, and as his eyes encountered mine, I detected the traces of tears upon his cheeks. My heart was full of love for my father, or childlike adoration it might have been called. I hurried to him and embraced him. The tenderness overcame his habitual self-restraint and he seemed to fall sobbing in my arms.

"My son," he finally whispered, "my days are drawing very fast to a close. The shock I experienced at Christ Church prepared me to believe I would die in some attack of paralysis. A slight aphasia occurred this morning. It, too, as suddenly disappeared. But these warnings cannot be neglected. I and you must at once make preparations for that future colloquy which we must endeavor to establish between ourselves, when I have left this earth and you yet remain upon it.

"I have been thinking a good deal on this subject and my reflections have resulted in this conclusion."

His voice had now resumed its usual melody and power, and we sat down while he turned the pages of Prof. Bain's little work entitled "Mind and Body." He read (I marked at the time the passage): "The memory rises and falls with the bodily condition; being vigorous in our fresh moments and feeble when we are fatigued or exhausted. It is related by Sir Henry Holland that on one occasion he descended, on the same day, two mines in the Hartz Mountains, remaining some hours in each. In the second mine he was so exhausted with inanition and fatigue, that his memory utterly failed him; he could not recollect a single word of German. The power came back after taking food and wine. Old age notoriously impairs the memory in ninety-nine men out of a hundred."

My father then continued: "It seems to me quite clear that our memory, at any rate, however little of our other mental attributes is engaged in matter, is quite constructed in a series of molecular arrangements of our nervous tissues. No doubt there is memory also in that subtle fluid that survives death, but, inasmuch as memory is so closely expressed in physical or material units or elements, does it not seem plain that as spirits we shall probably lose memory?

"The material structure in which it existed, which in a sense was memory itself, is dissipated by death. Memory disappears with it. But perhaps not wholly. Some shadow of itself remains. What will most likely be treasured then? The strongest, deepest memories only. Those which are so subjectively strong as to leave even in the spirit *flesh* an impression. In this same little book of Bain's this sentence occurs: 'Retention, Acquisition, or Memory, then, being the power of continuing in the mind, impressions that are no longer stimulated by the original agent, and of recalling them at after-times by purely mental forces, I shall remark first on the cerebral seat of those renewed impressions. It must be considered as almost beyond a doubt that the *renewed feeling occupies the very same parts, and in the same manner as the original feeling*, and no other parts, nor in any other manner that can be assigned.'

"It seems to me, my son, in view of all this, that, as the fondest hope of my life is to send back to you from wherever I may be, a message, and as we both believe the means must be something like this wireless telegraphy, I must imbed in my mind the whole system we have developed, and especially make myself almost intuitively familiar with the Morse alphabet. Beating, beating, beating upon my brain substance this ceaselessly reiterated mechanical language, it will become so incorporated, that even in the surviving mind I shall find its traces and be able to use it.

"So I have concluded to put aside almost everything else and think and live in the thought only of this coming experience. You understand me? You sympathize in this? Yes, yes, I shall get ready for this supreme experiment which may at last, to a long waiting world, bring some reasonable assurance that death does not end all. As I think of it, as I look forward to meeting your mother, the whole prospect of death grows wonderfully interesting and sublimely welcome. And yet, my son, you, you who have been so patient, so kind, giving up your life for my convenience and pleasure, I dread to leave you. But I will speak to you! Watch! wait! and at that instrument upstairs, which I know responded to some waves of magnetism crossing the oceans of space, I shall be heard by you in English words, opening up the mysteries of other worlds!"

He stopped in sheer exhaustion with his whole face charged with almost frantic ecstacy. It seemed to me so natural, nurtured in the same impossible dreams, that I saw nothing ludicrous in his hopes.

From that day on we gave ourselves up to telegraphing from our two stations, while my father again and again consulted models of our transmitters and receivers. This excitement lasted a long time and it did seem psychologically certain that in any disembodied condition my father would be likely to recall some important parts or all of this well learned lesson.

For years my father, as I mentioned before, in his astronomical studies, had limited himself to the study, photography and drawing of the surfaces of our planetary neighbors. Mars particularly fascinated him, for he had, by some illusion or accident of thought fixed his belief firmly that Mars represented his future post mortem home.

The progress of study of the physical features of Mars had been considerable. With these results my father and I were very familiar, had been in correspondence with certain astronomical centers with regard to them, and had even contributed something toward the elucidation of the problems thus presented.

In 1884, before the Royal Society, some notes on the aspect of Mars, by Otto Baeddicker, were read by the Earl of Rosse. They were accompanied by thirteen drawings of the planet and showed many features represented on the Schiaparelli charts. W.F. Denning in 1885, remarked upon "the seeming permanency of the chief lineaments on Mars, and their distinctiveness of outline." Schiaparelli confirmed his previous observations upon the duplications of the canals and Mr. Knobel published some sketches.

In 1886, M. Terby presented to the Royal Academy of Belgium notes on drawings made by Herschell and Schroeter, indicating the so-called Kaiser Sea. M. Perrotin at the Nice Observatory was able to redetect Schiaparelli's canals, which elicited the remark that "the reality of the existence of the delicate markings discovered by the keen-sighted astronomer of Brera seems thus fully demonstrated, and it appears highly probable that they vary in shape and distinctness with the changes of the Martial seasons."

These observations of M. Perrotin were detailed at length in the *Bulletin Astronomique*, and the distinguished observer called attention to the fact that these markings varied but slightly from Schiaparelli's chart, and indicated a state of things of considerable stability in the equatorial region of Mars. M. Perrotin recorded changes in the Kaiser Sea (Schiaparelli's *Syrtis Major*). This spot, usually dark, was seen on May 21, 1886, "to be covered with a luminous cloud forming regular and parallel bands, stretching from northwest to southeast on the surface, in color somewhat similar to that of the continents but not quite so bright." These cloud-like coverings were later more distributed and on the three following days diminished greatly in intensity. They were referred by Perrotin to clouds.

In March and April of the year 1886 a study was made of the surface of Mars by W.F. Denning in England. Mr. Denning's drawings corroborated the charts of Green, Schiaparelli, Knobel, Terby and Baeddicker. He found the surface of Mars one of extreme complexity, a multitude of bright spots in places, but with a general fixity of character which led him to believe that the appearances were not atmospheric. He indeed attributed to Mars an attenuated atmosphere and thought that some of the vagaries in its surface characters were due to variations in our own atmosphere He did not find the Schiaparelli canals as distinct in outline as given by that ingenious observer. He noted many brilliant spots on Mars and indicated the disturbing influences of vibrations produced by winds on the surface of our earth in connection with changes in the earth's atmospheric envelope.

In 1888 M. Perrotin continued his observations on the channels of Mars and noted changes. The triangular continent (Lydia of Schiaparelli) had disappeared, its reddish white tint indicating, or supposed to indicate, land, was then replaced by the black or blue color of the seas of Mars. New channels were observed, some of them in "direct continuation" with channels previously observed, amongst these an apparent channel through the polar ice cap. Some of these seemed double, running from near the equator to the neighborhood of the North Pole. The place called Lydia disappeared and reappeared. A strange puzzling statement was made that the canals could be traced straight across seas and continents in the line of the meridian. M. Terby confirmed many of these observations. Later the so-called "inundation of Lydia," observed by M. Perrotin, was doubted. Schiaparelli himself, Terby, Niesten at Brussels, and Holden at the Lick Observatory, failed to remark this change. These observers did not double the canals satisfactorily, but all agreed upon the striking whiteness and brightness of the planet.

M. Fizeau (1888) argued that the Schiaparelli canals were really glacial phenomena, being ridges, crevasses, rectilinear fissures, etc., of continental masses of ice. Again (Bulletin de l'Academie Royale de Belgique, June) M. Nesten averred that the changes on the surface of Mars were periodic.

In 1889, Prof. Schiaparelli reviewed what had been observed upon the surface of the planet in a continued article in *Himmel und Erde*, a popular astronomical journal published by the Gesellschaft Urania and edited by Dr. Meyer.

Some remarkable photographs taken by Mr. Wilson in 1890 were commented on by Prof. W.H. Pickering in the "Sidereal Messenger." They showed the seasonal variations in the polar white blotches.

In 1889 there reached us from Chatto and Windus of London a most entertaining book by Hugh MacColl, entitled "Mr. Stranger's Sealed

Packet." It was a work of fancy, ingeniously constructed upon scientific principles. It described a hypothetical machine, a flying machine, which was made up of a substance more than half of whose mass had been converted into repelling particles. Such a fabric would leave the earth, pass the limits of its attraction with an accelerating velocity and move through space. In such a way Mr. Stranger reached Mars. He found it inhabited by a people—the Marticoli—happy in a state of socialism, and with abundance of food manufactured from the elements, oxygen, hydrogen, carbon and nitrogen, with electric lights, phonetic speech, but without gunpowder or telescopes.

Its inhabitants had been derived from the earth by a most delightful scientific fabrication. A sun and its satellites in its course around some other center draws the earth and Mars so together that on some parts of the earth's surface the attraction of Mars would overcome that of the earth and gently suck up to itself inhabitants from the earth, who would not suffer death from loss of air, as the atmosphere of both bodies would be mingled.

These observations and this last scientific myth have some interest in view of the actual knowledge now vouchsafed to the world through my father's messages. I have very briefly reviewed them.

My father's premonitions were fully realized. He grew sensibly weaker as the months of 1891 passed. His mind became eager with the cherished expectation which grew day by day into a sort of a mild possession. It seemed to me that there was a moderate aberration involved in his deeply seated convictions, and when sometimes I saw him walking past the windows on the plateau with his head thrown back, his arms outstretched as if he were inviting the stars to take him and his murmuring voice, repeating some snatches of song, I felt awed and frightened.

My father was stricken with paralysis on September 21, 1892, became speechless the following day, but for a day thereafter wrote on a pad his last directions. Some of these were quite personal, and need not be detailed here. It was indeed pathetic to see his strenuous and repeated efforts to assure me that he remembered all the parts of the telegraphic apparatus, and his smile of saddened self-depreciation when he hesitated over some detail. At last he sank into a torpor with the usual stertorous breathing, flushed face and gradually chilled extremities. His last words were scrawled almost illegibly by his failing hand—"Remember, watch, wait, I will send the messages."

Miss Dodan came to the plateau and was helpful; to me especially. She kept up my breaking spirits, and her womanly tenderness, her brave grace, and the joy my loving heart felt in seeing her, enabled me to go through the trial of death and separation.

All was finished. My father was buried in Christ Church cemetery by his own request, although thus separated by a hemisphere from his wife.

* * * * *

A year had passed. I had received nothing. Mr. and Miss Dodan came to the observatory. They both were acquainted with the singular prepossessions which controlled both myself and my father, and I think Mr. Dodan was himself, though he admitted nothing, most curious and interested in the whole matter. Miss Dodan frankly said she was. But I know, to Miss Dodan's fresh, healthy, human life there was something weirdly repellent in this thought of communication with the dead. She thought of it with a nervous dread and excitement. It just kept me in her thoughts a little shrouded in mystery and superiority and closed a little the avenues of absolute confidence and peaceful self-surrender.

I had forgotten nothing, although at first an overwhelming sense of the uselessness of the attempt, the almost grotesque absurdity of expecting to hear from beyond the limits of the earth's atmosphere any word transmitted through a mechanical invention, upon the earth's crust, made me feel somewhat ashamed of my preparations, yet I arranged every portion of the receiver and exercised my best skill to give it the most delicate adjustment.

Whenever I had occasion to rest I either sent an assistant to the post, or kept on my pillow, adjusted to my ear, a telephone attachment to the Morse register, so that its signals might instantly receive attention. At length as time wore on I arranged a bell signal that might summon us to the register.

On the occasion of this visit by the Dodans I was in the loft at the receiver which was in a room to one side of that we called "the equatorial," where the telescope was suspended. I was as usual waiting for a message that never came, and my failing hopes, made more and more transitory by the brightness of the southern spring and all the instant present industry of the fields below me on the low-lands, seemed to dissolve into a mocking phantom of derisive dreams.

I stood up hackneyed and forlorn. Had I not done everything I could? Had I not kept my promise? I heard the voices below me; one, that musical tone, that made the color come and go upon my cheeks, and as I turned hastily to descend to them while the breathing earth seemed to send upward its powerful sensitizing odors that turn energy into languorous desire, and touch the senses with indolence; at that moment the Morse register spoke!

Could my ears have deceived me? No! It was running, running, running, intelligible, strong, definite; it seemed to me of almost piercing loudness, although just audible. I bent over, seized my pad and wrote. The Abyss of

Death was bridged! From behind the veil of that inexorable silence which lies beyond the grave came a voice—and what a voice! The clicking of a telegraphic register in signals, that the whole world knew and used. I was quiet, preternaturally so, I think, as I took down the message. I became almost aged in the intense rigidity of my absorption.

I was told the Dodans came up and saw me, heard the telltale clicks of the register, and unnoticed left me. Still I wrote on, unheeding the time. My assistants, pale with wonder, stood around me. The measured tappings were the ghostly voices of another world. This message began at 10 a.m., Sept. 25, 1893. It ended at 10 p.m. on the same day. It came quite evenly, though slowly, and was unmistakably intended to be inerrantly recorded, as indeed it was.

CHAPTER III

"My son," it began, "I am indeed in the red orb of light we have so often looked up to when we were together on the earth, and about which our wondering minds hazarded so many fruitless guesses. I have been here a short time, and now am able to return to you, by that cipher we so fortunately printed upon the tablet of memory, word of my existence.

"I can hardly describe to you my occurrence on this planet. I found myself here without any recollection of whence I had come, without a traceable thought of anything I had ever heard before.

"I was suddenly sitting in a high room, brilliantly lighted by a soft, tranquillizing radiance, listening to a chorus of most delicately attuned voices, indescribably sweet, penetrating and moving. Around me upon white ivory chairs arranged in an amphitheatre sat beings like myself, all looking outward upon a sloping lawn where were gathered beneath blossoming fruit trees an army, it seemed, of half shining creatures, unlike myself, singing these wonderful choruses.

"I have since learned that I did not reach Mars in that identical moment when I found myself sitting in the hall. I had come to it, as all disembodied spirits from the earth come to it at one receiving point, a high hill not far from the tropic of Mars. This hill, crowned and covered with glass buildings, is known as the hill of the Phosphori. Here, for nearly one of our months, the incoming souls, which are little more than a sort of ethereal fluid, presenting a form only observable by refracted light, or I should say polarized light, are bathed in a marvellously phosphorescent beam procured by absorption from the sun. These souls are intermingled in a chaotic stream that I may liken to the streaming currents of heated air in convection from a source of heat upon our earth, and this continuous tide is caught in a great spherical chamber or a series of chambers extending over five miles around the bald summit of this eminence.

"In these colossal chambers the phosphorescent light from enormous radiators beats incessantly through and through the slowly, oscillating, vibrating, revolving soul matter. And here the process of individualization is achieved. A soul, or many souls, are separated from the great tide, by flashing, under the bombardment of the phosphorescent blaze into shining forms. They assume a shape outlined by light, and just slightly subject to gravity from the atomic compression necessary to maintain their illumination, they fall lightly out from the domes of the spheres, touch the floors beneath, and are led away.

"In this way I found later I had arrived at Mars. When the spirits, thus shaped in light and otherwise almost immaterial and unclothed, emerge from the Hill of the Phosphori, they are taken along wide, white roads to some of the many chorus halls which fill the City of Light, where I am now, and from which I am sending this magnetic message. They remain for hours, even days and weeks in these halls listening in a sort of stupor or trance to beautiful music; for music is the one great recreation of the Martians, and is spontaneous, appearing as a vocal gift in beings who have never enjoyed its exercise on earth.

"Gradually under the influence of this musical immersion, as under the bombardment of the phosphorescent rays, a mentality seems developed; voice and language come, and the soul moves out of the concourse of listening souls, moved by a desire to do something, into the streets of the city. This is called, as we might say, the Act Impulse. From that time on the soul rushes, as it were, to its natural occupation. Its mentality, aroused by music, becomes full of some sort of aptitude, and it enters the avenues of its congruous activity as easily, as quickly, as justly as the growing flower turns toward the Sun wherever it may be.

"Let me present to you the curious scene my eyes encountered as I sat in the great Chorus Hall. I say my eyes. It is hard perhaps for you to realize what an organ can be in a creature, so apparently, as we are, little more than gaseous condensations. The physiology and morphology of a spirit is not an easy thing to grasp or define. I am yet ignorant upon many points. But dimly, at least, I may make your natural senses cognizant of it.

"You have seen faces and forms in clouds. How often you and I from Mount Cook on the earth have watched their changing and confluent lineaments in the clouds above the New Zealand Alps. It is the same way with Martian spirits. They are tenuous fluids, but the individual pervades them and a material response is evoked, and the light from their surfaces is so halated, intensified, or reduced as to form a figure with a head and arms and legs.

"In some way I imagine the organs are optical effects, ruled by mind, which is located in this luminous matter. Later I will describe the process of *solidification, the resumption of matter*, for these spirit forms slowly concrete into beings like terrestrial men and women. There is, therefore, a dual population here, the extreme newly transplanted souls, and the flesh and blood people, and between them the transitions from spirit to corpuscular bodies. But all this takes place in the City of Light. Elsewhere over the whole planet the spirits are seldom seen, but only the vigorous and beautiful race of material beings into which, they—the spirits—have *consolidated*.

"To return to my first experience in the Chorus Hall in the City of Light. I seemed to be in a great alabaster cage enormously large and very beautiful. Its shining walls rose from the ground and at a great height arched together. The front was a network of sculpture, it held the rising rows of what seemed like ivory chairs on which the motionless white and radiant assemblage were seated. The whole place glowed, and this phosphorescent prevails throughout the City of Light, just as it does in the Hill of the Phosphori, when we first landed in this strange existence.

"The music came from a field in front of the Chorus Hall, which held a wonderful array of beings who, while not radiant as we were, had a *lustrous* look over their smooth and lovely bodies, which were tightly clad in the palest blue tunics and leggings. These creatures were consolidated spirits. They are constantly augmented by new arrivals, and, as the number remains almost unchanged, as new arrivals appear, others leave and then move off from the City of Light into the vast regions of Mars outside and beyond the city.

"A word of explanation would make this all clear. The Hill of the Phosphori begins the transmutation of the psychic fluid which makes up the souls as they flow into Mars from space. At the Hill the very moderate condensation begins, just enough to bring them to the ground by gravity. The psychic fluid is susceptible to the light, absorbs and emits it, and so the spirit forms are shining like great *ignes fatui* on our old earth. The spirits thus individualize, pass in companies to the City of Light, and come to the huge chorus halls which surround the city on its outskirts, in the country margin.

"They reach these chorus halls by a sort of suasion produced apparently by their sympathy with music. Music and Light are the energies, which at first and measurably throughout all the latter days of Martian life, direct work and thought and being. The music is quite audible for long distances, especially in the direction of the Hill of the Phosphori where the spirits land. Drawn by it they move unconsciously toward the singing centers. Now there are perhaps a hundred of these chorus halls about the City of Light grouped in the direction of the Hill of the Phosphori, and the music is quite different in them. There are four principal sorts, the grave, the gay, the romantic and the harmonic. By their interior sympathy the kinds of spirits move to the choruses which afford the music they respond to and it is wonderful how infallibly this attraction acts.

"The bands separate and strings and lines of the phosphorized spirits train away without direction to the choruses that attract them, although only a sort of subdued and confused murmur reaches them from the halls.

"Throughout the first stages of life here, the spirits are somnambulous. They move and act unconsciously and in obedience to their imbedded instincts and tastes. Only, as under the influence of music and light and afterwards occupation, they are transmuted by consolidation into the fair material race, which outside of the City of Light controls the planet, does consciousness and curiosity and language arise. I sat a long, long time in the chorus hall, to which I was drawn, which produced *grave* music. I knew nothing, felt nothing, was but dimly cognizant of what was about me, but I thrilled with the music.

"I felt the process of condensation going on, and it was a process exquisitely blissful. Now and then, a spirit form would arise and step down the rising forms and go out, another and another, while as silently spirits from the Hill of the Phosphori would enter and take their seat and bathe in the almost unbroken surges of music that come from the field outside, from the multitude beneath the almond blossom laden trees. Movement is without volition in the spirit stage; attraction that follows a hidden impulse, that seems indescribable at first, directs them. It is only as the process of consolidation in the City of Light individualizes, that the spirits become, as you would say, human. But it is a humanity of great beauty. Material particles invade or transfuse them, replacing the diaphanous phosphorescent spirit fluid, and they grade into supple white and rosy figures, strong, strenuous and splendid.

"After remaining a long time, perhaps, in the chorus hall, I felt the restlessness that causes one after the other of the spirits to go out. I followed the solitary line out into the city, the solemn, swaying music still heard as I stepped out upon the broad steps which face the city. I was now more observant, something like sight and feeling and memory were slowly generated within me, and I noticed that whereas the arriving spirits moved like apathetic ghosts, those with whom I now was, turned with interest this way and that, seemed apprehending and alive.

"The spirits from the Hill of the Phosphori came on the broad avenues leading to the chorus halls like waifs of cloud driven by a zephyr, with no visible distention of parts, no leg, or arm, or head or body motion. Now they moved with some anatomical suggestions.

"I stood amid a colonnade of arches, the white shining columns rose around me to the high, shining roof, before me a long descent of steps, and beyond me and around on a softly swelling eminence was spread the City of Light. It was a marvellous picture.

"The City of Light is simple and monotonous in architecture, but its composition and its radiance quite surpass any earthly conception. The buildings are all domed and stand in squares which are filled with fruit trees, low bush-like spreading plants, bearing white pendant lily-like flowers or pink button-shaped florets like almonds. Each building is square, with a portico of columns, placed on rising steps, a pair of columns to each step. Vines wind around the columns, cross from one line of columns to another and form above a tracery of green fronds bearing, as it was then, red flowers, a sort of trumpet honeysuckle.

"The walls of the buildings are pierced on all sides with broad windows or embrasures, filled, it seemed, with an opalescent glass. Avenues opened in all directions, lined on both sides with these wonderful houses, which are made of a peculiar stone, veined intermittently with yellow, which has the property of absorbing and emitting light.

"It is indeed a phosphori as, if I recall it aright, the sulphides of barium, strontium, and calcium were upon our earth. Later I shall see the great quarries of this stone in the Martian mountains. Another strange feature in these Martian houses was the hollow sphere of glass upheld above each house. It is a sphere some six feet in diameter made up of lenses. It encloses a space in the center of which is a ball of the phosphorescent stone. During the day the rays of the sun are concentrated upon this ball of stone, and at night the stored-up sunlight is radiated into lambent phosphorescent light.

"It was the close of a Martian day that I felt the returning impact of volition and left the chorus hall. I emerged, as I said before, upon the broad platform with its colonnade of columns and arches and saw the city as the night drew on. It is difficult to put in words, my son, the wonderful effect.

"Each house built of this strange substance, which throughout the day had been storing up the energies of light, now, as the fading day waned, became a center of light itself. At first a glow covered the sides of the houses, the colonnade and dome, while the glass prisms above them sent out rays from their imprisoned balls of phosphori. The glow spread, rising from the outskirts of the city in the lower grounds to the summits of the hills where the sun's last rays lingered. It became intensified. The green beds of trees were black squares and the houses, pulsating fabrics of light between them. A slight variety of architecture in places was accentuated by diverse and varying lines or surface light.

"The whole finally blended and a sea of radiance was before me in which the beautiful houses were descried, the illuminated groves, and like enormous scintillations the glassy spheres—the Martians call them the *Plenitudes* above them. Many other developing beings were around me, and voiceless, mute, impassioned, with an admiration which we had as yet no adequate organs to express we gazed upon the throbbing metropolis, ourselves luminous spectres in the vast eruption of glorious light before, above, around us.

"As the night settled down the light grew more intense, more beautiful. I could discern the opalescent glasses in the houses sending out their parti-colored rays, patching the trees with quilts of changing colors, and far away there came, still unsubdued by the night, the continuous elation of music.

"All night, all day, the choruses kept on with intermissions, but the singers change. This musical facility is the mental or emotional characteristic of the Martian. There is more in music than you earthlings know or dream of. It is a part of the immortal fiber of men, and in Mars it *creates* matter, for the slow assumption of material parts, as I have said, is propagated and accomplished by music, and the parts thus made are the most perfect expression of matter the divine form of man or woman can know, I think. They are tuned to health, to beauty, to inspiration, but all of this you shall know.

"So I went down the steps into the city. I was with a group of spirits who noticed me, and whom I noticed, but as yet the listless, strange, doomed expression was on our faces, and though memory was beginning to light its fires within us, though the transmission of viewless particles of matter into our fluent bodies of spirit had begun, though mind and desire were awakened, not a word passed our shining lips, and we moved on in silence.

"The City of Light is often called in the Martian language also the City of Occupation, for here the forming spirits work. I have told you that as *consolidation*, through Music and Light, goes on, the aptitudes or tastes are awakened, and this first birth of desire in Mars carries the spirits off from their ivory seats in the Chorus Halls to the City, where like an animal ferreting its purpose by intuition, they seem impelled whither their needs are best satisfied.

"I now know that the City of Light is generally divided,—not exactly, but as association would naturally impel, into four quarters, the quarter of art, the quarter of science, the quarter of invention, the quarter of thought. This is simply that the artists, the scientific minds, the designers, and the philosophers are somewhat by themselves. The population of the City of Light is made up of a fair, white race of Martians, and of the forming spirits. As the forming spirits attain materialization through occupation, they may remain in the City or go out into the other cities, and into the country to work and live.

"Besides the quarters I have mentioned, there is the business section and the offices of the government.

"In the light of all I have learned since I came, I may at once explain something about the actual life and social organization of this strange world.

"The Martian world is one country. There are here no nationalities. The center of the country is in the City of Scandor, quite removed from the City of Light. Business is carried on as with you on the earth, but its nature and its physical elements vary, as you will see. There is a circulating medium, banks and business enterprises, but it is more veiled, more hidden, less, far less, insistent than with you. A great socialistic republic is represented in Mars, and the limits of individual initiative are very narrow. Still they exist.

"One prime element of difference is in the nourishment and the area of population. The Martian lives only on fruit, and he lives only a few degrees on either side of the Equator. All the businesses that in your earth arise from the preparation and sale of meat and all the various confections, disappear there, and also all the mechanism of house heating and lighting. Also there are no railroads, but innumerable canals, which form a labyrinth of waterways, and are fed from the tides of the great northern and southern seas.

"The business is largely agricultural, but in the cities the pursuit of knowledge still continues. There is, however, on Mars a much lessened intellectual activity than on the earth. It is a sphere of simplified needs and primal feelings exalted by acutely developed love of Music. Mars is the music planet. There are not on Mars newspapers, journals, magazines, books. The tireless production of these things on the earth has but one analogy in Mars, the publication of music scores, the recitation of poetry and symposia, and the great illustrated journal, Dia. But these things I will explain later.

"I wandered on that night through the city with other spirits. We went through the city streets in the radiance of the *Plenitudes* above the houses. The night air was blowing through the trees, and the city was filled with people. They were the Martians. We were scarcely noticed. In the City of Light the new arrivals are not questioned until they begin to "take shape," as they say here, and then they are closely examined, and their origin, if it can be traced, is written down and kept in great registers.

"The groups were moving in streams toward the higher ground, and as my companions were gradually separated from me and were lost like wisps of moving light here and there, I went on alone. I came up long, wonderful avenues between walls of light, regularly punctuated by the dark squares of trees, and the spherical radiations of the Plenitudes above the houses.

"The people about me seemed all young, or scarcely more than, as we say, in middle life. They speak less than the earth folk, and when they speak they utter very simple sentences, and seem very sincere. I often stood by little groups gathered at the corners of cross streets, and listened to their musical intonations. The language is vocalic and monosyllabic. It sometimes suggests a Mongolian tongue, but without the guttural clicks and coughs. The Martians are all gifted in music. It fills their lives.

"From point to point crowds were assembled about platforms where singing was in progress, and every now and then a man or woman in the street would sing loudly and passionately with such power and beauty that the impressionable Martians would follow the refrain of the song and the whole street for blocks and blocks would resound in waves of delightful melody. There are no mechanical modes of propulsion in the streets of the City of Light. *The Martians all walk.*

"I approached the top of the broad hill on which the City is built, and came suddenly out into a square filled again in its park-like center with trees. From amid these trees rose a massive building, which I instantly recognized as an observatory; the many round domes, as on earth, were unmistakable.

"I passed up the walks of the square to the building and entered it.

"It was illuminated by balls of phosphori in glass globes, and its cool, broad halls and stairways were, in the soft light, very beautiful. But their wonderfulness consisted in the insertion upon the walls of illuminated plans and maps of the heavens. These miniature firmaments were all afire, so that each opening, carefully graded in size to represent stars of the first or second or third magnitude, was filled with a beaming point of light, and I walked in these noble corridors between reduced patterns of the universe of stars. I can hardly tell you how astonished and entranced I was.

"I had for the first time since I reached the planet the impulse of speech, and I raised my hands with that motion of snapping the fingers, which you recall was characteristic of me on earth, and *spoke*. I cried, 'Here is my home.'

"As my hands dropped to my sides I felt resistance. I looked down upon myself and could behold the changing surfaces of my body. Under this completing stroke of volition the work begun upon the Hill of the Phosphori and the Chorus Hall in reducing the intangible spirit fluid to corporeal expression was now hastening to an end. I do not stop here to consider the reflections this suggests as to the nature of matter, those abstruse speculations we indulged in so often over the pages of Muir and Helmholz and Tait and Crookes.

"I had reached the ascending stairway, when my hand—for hand it now seemed to be—was taken in a friendly pressure, and I turned and saw a tall figure with a face of extreme nobility, somewhat scarred, I thought, dressed in the usual Martian attire of a flowing tunic and closely fitting body clothing. He said in English, 'You are from the earth as I am.'

"My son, how can I, in this dull, mechanical method of conversation with you, ignorant, indeed, whether the magnetic waves loaded with my message, are traversing or not the millions of miles of space to your ear, how can I make you realize the wonderful and blessed feelings of amazement and happiness that the stranger's words brought me. Here I was, a disembodied soul from Earth, which at that moment I only dimly recalled, undergoing the strange process of re-establishment in flesh and blood, and slowly appropriating those natural appetites which come with flesh and blood, a waif of spiritual being in the great voids of creation, impelled by some implanted power of affinity to this remote, strange, phantasmal and unreal place, overwhelmed in a stupor of confusion, like some awakening patient from the vertigo of a terrifying dream!

"I looked upon my friend, and in the rapidly rising flood of emotions that came with the acting members of my body, flushed and throbbing with excitement, and with a wild joy besides, I flung myself upon his neck and pressed him with arms that seemed once more those natural physical ties that have held upon my breast those I best loved on earth.

"The stranger led me slowly up the stairway and past great celestial spheres which filled the higher hallways, conducting me to a room at one corner of the great structure. The room was a singular and unique apartment. It consisted of a large central space, furnished with the usual ivory chairs, and a broad, massive center table, also of ivory, curiously inlaid with particles of the omnipresent *phosphori*, which gave out a liquid light and imparted indescribable chasteness and beauty to the carved ornaments upon them. The floor was dark, a leaden color, lustrous, however, like black glass, and made up in mosaic. Around the room were alcoves lit by lamps of the phosphori, and in each alcove a globe of a blue metal upon which were painted sketches like charts or maps. A chandelier of this blue metal was pendant from the ceiling, and in its cup-like extremities, arranged in vertical tiers, were round balls of the phosphori, glowing softly.

"Wide windows, unprotected by glass or sashes, just embrasures framed in white stone which everywhere prevails in Mars, looked out upon the marvellous City, which thus seemed a lake of glowing fires, over which, rising and refluent waves of light constantly chased each other to its dark borders, where the surrounding plain country met the City's edges. But throughout the distance I could trace lines of light marking highways or roads leading interminably away until quite extinguished at the optical limits of my vision.

"The walls of this beautiful room rose to an arched ceiling which was inlaid with this wonderful blue metal, seen in the globes, designed in scrolls and waving ribbons, and just descending upon the walls themselves in attenuated twigs and strings. The walls were bare and shining.

"My friend led me to one of the great windows and placed me in a chair. Drawing another beside me, placing his hand on mine, and leaning outward toward the burning splendor below us, above which in the still, clear heavens shone those stellar hosts you and I have so often watched with wonder, he said:

"'Ten Martian years ago I came to this world as you have come. As a spirit I entered the chambers on the Hill of the Phosphori. I sat in the Chorus Hall. I entered the City and slowly changed, as you are changing, into one of the Martian white people. I found my work, as you will, in this Patenta, for by that name in Mars is called this home of astronomy and physical philosophy. Here, amid telescopes and apparatus of experiment and investigation, I have spent the years, mapping with many others the skies, and above all beating the earth we left, as have many, many, whom you will meet, with magnetic waves, hoping against hope, that some response might be gained, some hint of that connection through space which the physicists of this planet expect, ere long, may make all the beings of the universe one great sidereal society.'

"He stopped and leaned away from me, perusing my face with interest. Words came to my lips, memory again asserted its triumphant declaration that I was the same being as had lived upon the earth, and with it the sudden turbulence of hope that she, your mother, whom we so often expected to regain, might, as I had, have reached this planet, too, and to me, renewed in youth, might come the glory and the joy of knowing her again.

"I turned to him and spoke: 'Kind friend, I am yet dazed and stricken with the marvellousness of my being here. It seems but a short time, a lapse of even a day, that I bade good-bye to my son on the death-bed in my home on earth. I am too tormented with wonder to speak to you much. I can tell all I know of myself in a little while. But now as I grow stronger, tell me of this new world, and oh! give me, sir, food. I feel the quickening fevers of appetite and desire.'

"The man arose and left the room. In a few moments he returned followed by a boy and a young woman bearing a basket. They spread a yellow cloth upon a small ivory table and set down two plates of the bright blue metal; upon one they placed a pile of small round cakes and on the other a number of red and yellow gourd shaped fruits. At a signal from my companion I arose and sat at the table.

"He remained at the window and continued: 'While you break your long fast, let me tell you what I know about this new world which will now be your home for a long time. You will learn all, but I am not watching tonight. In seeing you and hearing the familiar English speech I am moved myself by currents of retrospection; my earth home comes back to me. I will satisfy your curiosity, and, you in turn, must tell me what has happened in the old home.'

"He paused; from the streets of the city rose a sacred song. It came like a slowly increasing torrent of sound, soft and low, rising with impetuous fervor until it seemed to engulf us in its melodic tide. Individual tones were heard in it, but its solidity and mass were most impressive. I shook and trembled beneath the impact of its vibrations; in its surging glory of sound I became fully reincarnated. I awoke naked and ashamed. The man saw my confusion. He hurried to a niche in the wall and handed me the tunic of the Martians with its girdle of blue cord and its cap and shoes of the blue metal exquisitely wrought and light. I put them upon me and lifting the cakes and the mellow-soaked pears to my lips, listened.

"'The Martians,' he continued, 'are both a natural and supernatural race. The natural race are largely prehistoric, though many yet exist; the supernatural race are made up of beings from other worlds and a great majority come up from the earth. How reincarnation first began on Mars is unknown, though the natural people, the Dendas, have traditions about it, vague and contradictory. It must have been slow. The supernatural people thus brought to Mars have created its civilization, discovered the phosphori, and established Music, which is so much of their life, and accelerated in the way you have learned the process of materialization.

"'They built this City of Light from phosphorescent stone quarried from the Mountains of Tiniti. Formerly the spirits came helter skelter to Mars all over its surface and went wandering about, helped to reincarnation by the various villagers or citizens. The great new improvement in the last half century has been the creation of the receiving station at the Hill of the Phosphori, the building of the Chorus Halls, and the establishment of the City of Light. Light draws the spirits, and though spirits reach other points of Mars, the centralization of Light here, draws most of them to this side. The Martians are not immortal. They vanish in time.

"'As reincarnated all spirit becomes young but nourishment has undergone a change. The physiological process is singular. I need not dwell upon it. Evaporation replaces defecation. Love enters the Martian world, but it has lost much of the earthly passion. The physiological effects are also different. There are no children here.

"'We live in the tropical regions mostly of Mars, and the polar and north temperate zones are empty. The natural Martian races are found more plentifully there. They are strong and small and work under the supervision of the supernaturals. They are like the earthlings and eat meat. Our food is bread and fruit. Our language does not lend itself to composition; it only sings. Literature, as we knew it on earth, does not exist here. The natural Martians have tales and stories and plays and some books. These things no longer interest the supernaturals. Our life is quite simple, almost expressionless, except for the power of our music. The souls from different parts of the earth recognize each other and converse in human language, but, unless practiced, it is forgotten and our euphonies take its place. I have used my earth language with a friend and still speak English well.

"'We have art here, but it is almost wholly sculpture and architecture and design. Color, except in glass, does not greatly please the Martians and there are few painters. They survive from other worlds, but cannot secure pigments, and draw only in black and white for the most part. They are cartoonists, as we would say, on the earth. But we grow fruits and flowers, the former in varieties and richness unknown upon the earth and the latter in delicate tints with blues and yellows, the only primary strong tints the Martians admire.

"'Mechanical invention is discouraged, except as it assists astronomy. Astronomy is the great profession. Cars, railroads and conveyances, as you say on earth, do not exist. We walk or sail and float upon our canals. Our industry is agriculture and building. Architecture is studied and advanced beyond all you have ever known on the earth. Mars is filled with beautiful cities. Its whole government consists in a council at the City of Scandor, from which representatives issue to its various departments. One is here in the City of Light. His motives are always just. There are no parties, for there are no policies. Life is so simple. Beauty and knowledge only rule us. Character, as you, as I, knew it on the earth, does not exist. There are no temptations, and we live as children of Light, in a sort of childhood of feeling, with great gifts of mind. But even living is noble. There is indeed rivalry. Yes, envy is with us. We worship God in great temples in services of song. Sermons are never heard.

"'In this city the great designers live, also the men who work at the deep problems of life and thought and matter; and the sculptors. It is the next largest city to Scandor. Scandor is far away. I never saw it. Glass work is done here and throughout Mars. Making the blue metal which you see, quarrying stone and ore and coal for the smelters and glass factories, the fabrication of dress material and fabrics for houses, making our boats and canal ships, cutting down the forests in the Martian highlands, cultivating fruits and flowers and the great wheat fields are the chief industries, and there are lesser lines of work, as the potteries and the instrument makers.

"'There are no industries in the City of Light. It is employed as I told you. Its population is constantly changing, for spirits like you are reincarnated here, and these new multitudes come and go. To-morrow, the ships on the canals will carry many away. The spirits, as you did, when they enter the city, wander as they will; they enter the houses, the workshops, the laboratories, everything in obedience to their instinctive choice. The people of the City of Light are therefore largely engaged in caring for them as they fall into bodily forms, clothing, feeding, housing them.

"'Each householder and all citizens report to the Registeries what spirits have come to them, and whence they came, and the great diversion and entertainment of our people is to listen to the stories of other worlds, which these new arrivals bring. Memory does not survive long and they soon forget their past history. It is best so, except in fugitive and dreamlike fragments, unless they are great.

"'According to their desire or aptitudes, the spirits are sent away when Martianized to the different parts of Mars, and many stay here with us in the workshops and laboratories.

"'Besides Music, the people of Mars delight in recitation, and in the City of Scandor I hear there are great theatres or public places where recitations and concerts and even noble operas are held. Many of these are brought to us by great spirits from other worlds, their own works in poetry or prose or music. In Scandor there are great orchestras with all the instruments we had upon the earth, and the paper, Dia, is published there, which is read everywhere in Mars. There are few books, no schools in the common sense. The thinkers have assemblies and there are announcements and explanations of discoveries.

"'Our life in many ways is like the life on earth, but less active, more contemplative, and sin and money-making are almost absent. The wicked of all sorts have one fate; they are fired off the planet. We can overcome the attraction of gravitation by our Toto powder. These executions are strange to earth eyes. You will see them. The Toto powder is also a motive power.

"'We have a medium of exchange, silver, and there are rich and poor with us, but no poverty. There can be no armies nor navies. The government carries on extensive works of improvement and keeps the canals and pays its laborers. The government supports this City of Light and the people here are paid for the number of spirits they care for and assist. Happiness reigns on Mars, but it is a pensive happiness. We never, because of the singular physiology of our bodies, can know the boisterous and passionate joys of earth, neither do we know many of the ills of the flesh. We have sickness and there are accidents. We have a death, but it is like evaporation. We decline again after a long life to the spirit stage and vanish. So there are partings here, and the old sadness of the end as on earth; but the gaiety of children, the ambition of youth, the devotion of parents is unknown.'

"His voice sank, he bent his head upon his hands, and a sort of tremor ran through him, and when again he looked upon me his eyes shone with moisture, and the hot tears ran down his cheeks. Memory might be fleeting on Mars, but the loved ones of the earth were yet remembered, and the abysses of the eternal void of space could never be crossed by the wave of speech or recognition. This was the pathos of the Martian life.

"I was shown by him, as the slowly arising sweetness of fatigue showed itself within me, to a bedchamber of charming simplicity. The graceful bedstead of the blue metal was covered with snowy covers, curtains hung at the windows also white. The furniture of the room was of a sort of pale, red wood obtained in the great Martian forests where the trees known as the Ribi grow, whose leaves and flowers have a pink tint, which in seasons of fruitage is more intense, and present enormous areas of extraordinary beauty.

"This room was at the top of one of the many branching wings of this composite astronomical laboratory. To reach my room we walked through hallways all illuminated with the phosphorescent glowing balls while the radiant patterns in the walls shone also with a pale beauty. These balls possess a wonderful lighting power and besides their self-illumination can be stimulated into the most intense brilliancy by electric currents with which the Martians are profoundly acquainted. The electrical displays on Mars surpass description and the waves of magnetism I am now utilizing to send to you these messages are ten miles in amplitude.

"I fell asleep, quickly lulled into an almost death-like slumber by the cadence of innumerable fountains. Near the *Patenta* is the Garden of Fountains, which I shall tell you about in another message. It was the plash and rivulous current of these water courts that brought on sleep.

"I awoke when the Martian dawn was coming on. Slumber had given me the last reassurance of identity of body, and I awoke with a delightful sense of health and youth. I stood at the wide window near my bed and gazed out upon the yet luminous City of Occupation. The picture was of surprising strangeness and beauty. Far off, until melting into the encroaching edges of an outer blackness, the City extended its folds and surfaces of light. The streets were empty, the music of the Chorus Halls stilled. Here and there, a spirit was moving slowly through the streets, a half-made Martian; a breeze soft and salubrious stirred the thickly leaved trees and the firmament shone with the larger stars, beginning to pale before the rising sun. As the sun rose higher, the effulgence of the City died away, the light of the same great orb which brings the dawn to you, covered with its rays the white and glorious City, the music seemed again revived, and from the doorways of the houses I could see forms issuing, while far off the Hill of the Phosphori raised its glass domes in the air, where the homogeneous tide of spirit was undergoing differentiation, as we might say, into separate cognizable, discreet beings. An unspeakable delight filled me. I felt the power of mind and with it the radiant energy of manhood."

No more words came. The message ended. Not a motion or sound succeeded this wonderful trans-abysmal dispatch.

Well, here, at last, was the long expected, impossible, amazing reality. When I had deciphered the last word, when I had it borne fully in upon me, the significance of it all, I turned to the one natural effort to answer this Martian communication. I sent out from the battery of our transmitter the longest wave of magnetic oscillation I could emit. The message was simple: "Have received all. Await more. Transmission perfect."

CHAPTER IV

Again for weeks I watched the station. My assistants relieved me, and amongst them was now included Miss Dodan. It was only a few days after the Dodans found me at the register, absorbed in receiving my father's message, that Miss Dodan called. She ran toward me at the open door of the station, her face fixed in an anxious expression of half-alarmed expectation.

"Did you really, Mr. Dodd, hear anything? Is it true that something came from your father. Oh, tell me, can it be possible?"

I took her clasped hands in my own, looked into her face and told her everything. She was the first visitor to the station since the day of the marvellous experience. My assistants had promised secrecy, which I reinforced effectively by doubling their salaries. I felt I ought not to have revealed this thing to Miss Dodan, and when in the first impulse of confidence everything so unwittingly passed my lips, I took her arm in mine and walked out upon the broad plateau toward the opposite end where our smaller experimenting station had been built.

"Miss Dodan," I said, "I am going to ask a great favor of you."

"Yes," she answered, half musingly, for the tremendous fact I had related had half robbed her of her consciousness of passing things.

"I want you solemnly for the present to promise me not to reveal the strange thing I have told you. It would hardly be believed. No, I am sure it would be laughed at, and I would become in the eyes of everyone a foolish, impossible dreamer. This would give me a deep sorrow. My father's name would be dragged into the mire of this common ridicule. You revered my father."

I bent more closely over her, I felt her breath upon my cheeks, her eyes seemed fixed in mine, and then I did what I had never done before, I kissed the lips of a woman and it was also the lips of the woman I loved. There was no resistance, no withdrawal; a tremor—was it pleasure?—seemed to disturb her for a moment and again I kissed her. This time with a quiet effort toward release she separated herself from me, and while I still held her hands, our walk stopped and we faced each other, just where looking westward the spires, and flocking houses of Christ Church came fully in view.

"Miss Dodan," I began, fearful to use her first name through a reluctance that was itself the expression of the deep love I bore her, "Miss Dodan, I may for some time yet be engaged in this now imperative work. I cannot, you know, now leave it. It is the most marvellous thing the world has ever known. It means so much to me, indeed to us all. These messages are erratic—fitful. I have now waited for weeks for a renewal of these strange communications and there is nothing. But in the midst of this, a distracting love for you seems to unnerve and torment me. I beg you to wait until those days may come when I can show you all the devotion I yearn now to give you, but must not, for every moment that voice may reach me from beyond the grave, and I would be recreant to the most sacred obligations, and deep responsibilities that seem now to shape themselves before me, to our common humanity, if I forfeited an instant of inattention. I beg you to remember all this and wait, wait, until the depthless power of my love for you can be made clear."

I would have sunk upon my knees in the abasement and passion of my desire for her, had she not suddenly drawn me to her, flung her arms about my neck and placed her head where—well, I am no connoisseur in love scenes—but that day Agnes Dodan, without a syllable of sound gave her heart to me.

We passed back in silence, and when she left me the fluttering handkerchief that had so often waved back its salutation on the winding distant road was now in my hands, and its signals sent by me came to her from the plateau. It was the simple pledge of our mutual love, a pledge that even now as I prepare these last pages of a manuscript that is a testament to the world, soothes my pain and renews the happiness of that day, forever and forever lost.

The next message came a few days after my interview with Miss Dodan. It was a rainy day in November—the spring time of that Southern land. The register was heard by one of my assistants, Jack Jobson, a man who had unremittingly taken my place when I was absent, and who seemed more than anyone else dazed and wonder stricken over the experience we had. He came running to me, a wild terror in his face, exclaiming, "It's going again, sir. Hurry! It's running slow." I sprang upstairs, and before I had reached it heard the telltale clicks. It was not altogether a sheltered position, and as I reached the table I felt the bleak and chilly air penetrating the crevices of the window, a raw ocean breeze that in a few instants crept through my bones. But I was again unconscious of everything; that marvellous ticking obliterated all thought of earth, its affairs, accidents, dangers, loves, hopes, despairs, all forgotten, swallowed up in the immeasurable revelation I was about to receive.

The second message began at about 4 o'clock in the afternoon of November 25, 1893, two months exactly after the first. Its very opening sentences I failed to get. It lasted late into the morning of the next day. The strain of taking it was somehow singularly intense upon me. I was taken from the table the next morning unconscious. I had fainted at the close. It began, as I received it, a few opening sentences having been lost:

"...was sent to you I was in the City of Light, and now I am in the City of Scandor.

"The morning of that wonderful night in which I became a flesh and blood Martian, strong and young and beautiful, dawned fair. My friend came for me, and we went together to the great 'Commons' of the Patenta, a superb hall where all the professors, investigators, and students in the great Academy sit at many tables. This huge dining room is at the center of the group of buildings which make up the Patenta. Corridors lead into it from the four sections of the Patenta, and as we entered, from the different sides there were many men and some women taking the ivory chairs at the side's of the long tables of marble, on which rose in beautiful confusion of color crowded vases of fruits.

"Surrounding the room are niches instead of windows, and in each niche one noble symbolic figure in white or colored marble.

"Light fell in a torrent of glory through the faintly opalescent glass compartments of the ceiling, from which, at the intersection of the broad and long rafters of blue metal, hung chandeliers formed in branching arms with cup-like extremities, and holding spheres of the omnipresent *phosphori*.

"I stood a moment with my companion at the entrance of the great dining room, and watched the groups and individual arrivals, as they assorted themselves into companies or engaged in some short interchange of greetings. It was a very beautiful scene. The faces of all were wonderfully clear and strong, and in the commingling of forms, the bold, intellectual features of some, the more rare, delicate outlines of other faces, the flowing of the graceful tunics and robes, the pleasant, musical confusion of voices, with the quick, glancing movements of attendants, the heaped up chalices and baskets, vases and broad spreading plates of fruit, the many carelessly arranged and profuse bunches of radiant flowers in tall receptacles of glass or alabaster, in all this, with the strong, simple architectural features of the Hall, the eye and mind and senses seemed equally stimulated and satisfied.

"Amongst the glorious throng my companion pointed out to me many of those great men and women whom I seemed to know by their writings and portraits when on the earth. At one table sat Mary Somerville, Leverrier, Adams, La Place, Gauss and Helmholz; at another Dalton,

Schonbeim, Davy, Tyndall, Berthollet, Berzelius, Priestly, Lavoisier, and Liebig; here were groups of physicists—Faraday, Volta, Galvani, Ampere, Fahrenheit, Henry, Draper, Biot, Chladini, Black, Melloni, Senarmont, Regnault, Daniells, Fresnel, Fizeau, Mariotte, Deville, Troost, Gay-Lussac, Foucault, Wheatstone, and many, many more. At a small table immediately beneath a dome of glass, through whose softly opaline texture an aureole of light seemed to embrace them, sat Franklin, Galileo and Newton. It would be impossible to describe to you my amazement at the astonishing picture.

"It almost seemed as if the air vibrated with the excitement of its impact and use, as these giant minds conversed together. Endowed again with youth, scintillating, brilliant, the flush of a semi-immortality impressed upon their faces, which again bespoke the eminence of their intellects, in picturesque and effective, almost pictorial groupings, this wondrous gathering filled me with new rapture. My comrade led me to other branching halls similarly occupied. Chemists were here conspicuous— Chevreuil, Talbot, Wedgewood, Daguerre, Cooke, Fresenius, Schmidt, Avogadro, Liebig, Davy, Berthollet, and many, many more.

"It formed an equally striking scene. I turned to my companion and asked him how it was that the mathematicians, chemists, physicists, astronomers, were so crowded together. He said, 'The Patenta covers, with all its buildings, a space about one mile square, and here in laboratories and in the great observatories these men have flocked because of a sympathy in their tastes and talents. Although astronomy is the great profession, and, as I will show you, the marvels of the Universe are being more and more fully known, yet the study of the elements and the laws of matter is popular and also followed unremittingly. It is true that we know these people are from your earth; they have reported all that to the Registeries, to whom I will soon conduct you; they yet retain strong memories of the earth, though it is confined more largely to knowledge than to experience. In some, the Martian life and habit has almost obliterated their earthly notions and designs. It is singular that of the scientific workers of the earth the astronomers, physicists, and chemists alone reach Mars. The biologists, zoologists, botanists, geographers, and geologists rarely are booked at the Registeries as coming from the Earth. Their lives may be prolonged elsewhere, they seldom reach us.

"'There are some exceptions. The plants of Mars are numerous, its rocks and animal life curious, and they are well understood. A few doctors from the earth are here, but medicine and surgery are not so much needed, yet in the study of life our philosophers have made great strides. Your thinkers and poets, artists, composers, dramatists, musicians, come here, but of all the wonderful students of Nature the earth has produced, as far as I know or have heard, Lamarck and Agassiz, Owen, and Cuvier alone have been reincarnated on our globe. And the warriors and generals of the earth are unknown here.'

"We had reached a table unnoticed, unheard. There was a constant rush of words about us. The melodic charm of the Martian tongue, like the soft vocalization of Italian pleased me. If the Martians are without books or papers, they possess all the resources of conversation. Animation, pleasure, salutation, cheerfulness and joy was everywhere, the perfume of flowers filled the air, the shafts of sunlight broken into the most enticing iridescence filled the great noble rooms with lovely colors, and the clear white tables, beautifully spread with fruit, seemed to chasten appetite into something ethereal and rare.

"As we stood an instant at our places the people arose, and from some distant and concealed place, so situated I afterwards learned, as to gain access to all the dining halls, there came a swell and burst of jubilant music. It was so fresh and free and bewitching in its glee and ringing cadences, so consonant and accordant with the glad and illustrious feeling of the place and time, that my heart seemed to leap within me; and then it softened, and changing into notes of melodic gravity, ended in a splendid outcry of soaring, piercing notes—the salute to the morning. Long after the voices had finished, the rolling notes of an organ continued the loud outburst.

"As we sat down, the conversation was again resumed and I noted then the singular clearness and suavity of this Martian language. I must hasten my narrative. I have so much to tell you. We ate the great cereal of Mars— the Rint—a delicious food, in which, as it seemed to me, the substance of a sort of rice was mingled with a creamy exudation in all of which was enclosed the flavor of the orange and the peach. This, with a fruit, a kind of milk, and many wines, forms the nourishment of the Martians. The fruits are most various, and every hidden or patent fancy of the gourmet seems elicited or satisfied in them. I cannot now describe them even if I recalled them. One commended itself to my taste strongly, a sort of nodular banana, holding a fragrant nucleus, like a large strawberry immersed in a savory juice, and coated with a rind stripped from it by the hand. It is of most stimulating qualities. It is called Ana.

"Few implements are in use; the Rint is taken in short spoons and the fruit is usually manipulated with the fingers. The milk and wine are drunk from the most ingeniously devised and ornamented glasses, napkins of the Tofa weed are used, a pale green cloth, and large bowls of acidified water in which floats a morsel of soap are served at the end of meals. Great variety prevails, and individual fancy, taste, desire, or invention sway as with you on earth.

"The breakfast over, the companies arose and moved out in clusters and trains to the avocations of the day. Many of these workers in the Patenta have houses throughout the city, while others living singly congregate in the numerous apartments, and enjoy these commons. The extraordinary assemblage I saw here is repeated in the other great communal halls where the artists, philosophers and inventors congregate. But the Halls are of quite different construction in each quarter of the City.

"Accompanying or associated with these Halls are the Courts of Announcement and Recreation. Here lectures, conferences, entertainments, are given, and the people of the City flock in droves not infrequently accompanied by numbers of the new Spirits who here are often enabled to gain their final solidification; '*Gell*' as the Martians say.

"My companion led me out of the Hall. Men and women were moving slowly in various directions and as we made our way over the campus and between the many noble buildings I saw many of the lambent spirits half emergent into fleshly shapes accompanied by the watchers, who are in great numbers in the City, carrying over their arms the white and blue dresses with which to clothe them as the spirits fall into solid forms.

"Amongst these buildings I easily noted the marvellous observatories where objectives twenty feet in diameter are used with which the astronomers actually discern the life of our earth. The reports they make from week to week of their inspection of the Solar system, and of the commotions, changes, births and demolition of Stars, are the sensations of Mars. These Reports are read aloud in the Halls of Announcement and Recreation. But astounding beyond belief, they photograph the surfaces of these distant bodies, and report in moving pictures the disturbances of the cosmic universe. No wonder that the whole Mind, as it were, of Mars is concentrated on the fabulous results of their cosmic studies.

"We descended from Patenta Hill in an avenue that led between the white columned houses with their spheres of Phosphori and their umbrageous squares around them. It was a season of flowers, though I understood that by the use of fertilizing injections the number of flowers in a shrub and even in an herb can be here greatly multiplied. The windows of the houses were open and their sills crowded with blossoms. The use of the red blossoming vine was strangely extravagant. In many cases it had thrown its branches over an entire house, clambering over the roof and encircling the phosphoric cage, so that the white house was dissected by its twigs and tendrils, while the red honeysuckle flowers depended in clusters from the walls, the roof gutters, and the light house globes above them.

"The Court of the Registeries was a long low structure made of the prevalent white stone with a roof of what seemed to be red copper. It was built upon one of the canals which here enter the city and formed one side of a long pier or dock to which and from which interesting little boats were constantly approaching and as constantly departing.

"A hum of business and everyday work surrounded the place, and it seemed refreshing to note the stir and bustle of affairs. Streams of people were entering the Court as we arrived. They were inhabitants and watchers bringing the new incarnations to the Registeries to have their origin recorded if they could recall it. Indeed many spirits fail utterly to remember their former condition, and happen, as we might say, upon Mars, unexplained and inexplicable. They even are without speech and learn the Martian language as a child learns to talk.

"We pushed in with the jostling crowd, and even as I entered I could hear the murmurous chant of the Chorus Halls, borne hither-ward on the morning wind. It now seemed a long time, although but one day apparently had elapsed since I sat, a trail of luminous ether, undergoing the strange process of materialization.

"How incredible it all was, how incomprehensible. I pinched myself until I could have cried out with pain, and at that very instant a voice saluted me, calling me by name and a rushing figure encountered me. I stood transfixed. Before me was Chapman, the mechanic, workman, and photographer for Mr. Rutherford, in New York in the seventies, a man whom I knew well, from whom I had learned much, and whose skill helped so largely in the production of Rutherford's negatives of the Moon. My repulsion was over in an instant. I clasped him heartily. It seemed so good, so human, to embrace something in this strange world. An equal resistance met my own. We were indeed substance.

"'Mr. Dodd,' exclaimed my old acquaintance, 'are you here? This is wonderful. Have you just become one of us? What luck! what a great providence for me! I am in the observatory. Must sail to-morrow to Scandor to report a sudden confusion in Perseus. They call it here *Pike*. You shall go with me. I have a long leave of absence I will show you many marvels. And you can tell me everything about Tony. He was a baby when I knew you.' Turning to my smiling companion, he spoke in Martian, of which to give you some semblance I cipher these words: 'Aru meta voluca volu li tonti tan dondore mal per vuele vonta bidi ami.'

"I returned Chapman's hearty salutation. I yet retained the human speech of earth and I was struck with the miraculous incident that in the planet Mars, in a populous city, I was addressing a friend in the English tongue.

"But the joy of it was inexpressible. Oh, the sweetness of old acquaintanceship in strange, and as here, impossible surroundings! I gazed on him with unspeakable curiosity. I talked to him just to hear my own voice and his in response, to realize if words were still words with the old meaning, if the intangible mutation I had undergone was a reality, if I was indeed alive, if my lungs and throat, the configuration of my mouth, the vocalic impact of the air, was a fact, a sound, a meaning, or whether it all was some phantasmagoria, beautiful and fair indeed, to be dispelled with a shock of annihilation.

"No! we were breathing, sensate things, were human kin and kind. The sudden vertigo sent me throbbing, like a stricken animal, against the high pillars of the room we had entered, and a reflex tide of emotion swept over me in a storm that shook me with convulsive sobs.

"My companion handed me a black wafer. I took it, it dissolved, a fierce acridity seemed formed in my mouth, and in an instant I felt strong and bold.

"The Registeries were offices in the alcove-like openings in the sides of this very long building. In the same building were the Courts, which are few, and here the rooms for the reception and storage of supplies for the City. The Hall of Registeries is prolonged into a series of huge buildings extending along the walls of the Canal.

"I was led by my unknown friend and Chapman to one of these recesses on which I recognized a globe of our earth with its continents in relief. Here upon simple tables were spread great bound books made up of thick creamy leaves of white paper. These were the Registers. The original home, planet, world, or star, from which each emigrant spirit had departed was, as far as possible, determined, and appropriately recorded. The details of their lives were inquired into, the condition and history of the sphere they had left examined, and thus by the revision and comparison of these narratives the history of the various worlds was in a fair way known, almost as accurately as their present inhabitants knew them.

"The alcoves of the Registeries were really ample rooms. Cases holding voluminous records were ranged upon their walls; maps, charts, even paintings and drawings, as made by the arriving spirits hung upon the walls, and in broad albums were gathered the portraits, in small size, of the incarnated persons. The Registeries were young men who, from long intercourse with the affairs and occupants of each of the different extra-Martian bodies, whence spirits came, had become familiar with their languages and circumstances and avocations.

"The keeping, indexing, compiling, illustration, of these extraordinary records is a difficult and inexhaustible task.

"The results are often reproduced to the Martians in lectures, bulletins, or in sections of the great newspaper Dia.

"The young men approached us as we entered the room, and after saluting my guide and also Chapman with the Martian cry, Tintotita, led me to a chair, and giving me one of the black wafers, whose acidity had a short time before so vigorously renewed my consciousness, began their inquiry.

"The photograph of each visitor is taken, and a process quite like our collodion or wet process is used. The portraits are more permanent than with the perishable dry plates. It is a curious thing to learn that for 100 years these records and pictures have been taken, and that there are on Mars hosts of unidentified spirits, who entered its wondrous precincts before that time.

"The duration of life in Mars is very various. There seems here an undiscovered law, and a group of observers in Mars are to-day trying to penetrate this mystery. It is asserted that there is evidence that Egyptians of the ante-Christian epoch are to-day living in Mars, but their identification is now almost impossible. On the other hand, it is a fact ascertained and recorded that in one hundred years many Martians die, while others scarcely survive the ordinary limit of our human life on earth. This gives a great interest to Martian society. Here for ages have possibly flown disembodied spirits from our earth; in their reincarnation they have assumed the features and faculties of youth; they have also, under changed conditions of life, and moderated functions and activity in living, been physically, perhaps mentally, modified. Their own memory of their past on Earth, however vivid, and then in exceptional beings, has slowly disappeared or left only vague cloud-like waverings and congeries of reminiscences.

"So that great human souls that have entered Mars in the early centuries of our earth's historic periods may be living here almost unrecognized. They have drifted into occupations suitable to their genius in some of the many great cities, and no vestige of their past remains. The system of the Registeries is scarcely a century old, and while now from the marvellous industry and persistence of the investigators, the great ones of the neighboring worlds, and even the most obscure are in some cognizable way identified, yet from the long ages before that there is almost no authentic registration.

"This is more to be regretted as the law of life on the planet might then be better formulated. Essentially it seems necessary for existence here to be in unison with the conditions; contentment means longevity. Of course, the remarkable men and women I saw at the Patenta were all well known. They had made themselves known, and not only were their earthly names and lives put down on the pages of the Registers, but all their knowledge had been as inquisitively and scrupulously impressed. Nor is this all. From many worlds and earths there is flowing constantly to this planet new, strange, wonderful beings. Here is a cosmos of races, tastes, nationalities, destinies, civilizations, and instincts, from whose amalgamated and fused vortices of tendency this marvellous life has been formed.

"However completely the mere memory of detail vanishes, the traits of nature remain, and these mingling beings present a kaleidoscope of contrasted or blending talents. But union of beings comes in here as in our States to combine all together and create this unique expression of social beauty, tenderness, scientific power, progress and spiritual exaltation. Marriage is here as with us, and love holds its deathless sway among the white and noble Martians as on earth, while the affection of friendship seems to weave every atom of society to every other atom in a social texture over which only moves the refining powers of thought and aspiration.

"Mars does indeed seem a sort of Paradise, for it is quite certain that the best, the truest, the deeper and emphatic souls come here; and while a sort of sin or social incompatibility is found here, and there are crimes, and while death and sickness and accidents occur here, as I have told you, yet these things have a moral or mental, rather than physical expression. At least, in a great measure, and they are rare. No! accidents of matter pertain to Mars; its materiality is complete. As I send this to you I feel my warmth, the heat of my body, the expiration of my breath, the movements of my eyes, the beating of my heart, all, all, these bodily phenomena seem unchanged—their physiology is changed, their corporate reality seems the same, their corporeal consequences are different. But I cannot explain clearly this to you. Do I know it clearly myself?

"I was questioned by the Registeries, both of whom had come from the earth, though in them, as in all the less highly endowed, memory was fading. Because of this, Registeries quickly succeed each other, since the later arrivals from the other worlds are better adapted to elicit the information needed from the new spirits. And this applies to other worlds, to Mercury and Venus, etc., whose Registeries are, so far as possible, appointed from previous occupants of those spheres.

"The larger, far larger percentage of spirits come from the three planets, Mercury, Venus and the Earth; but there are singular inexplicable arrivals from distant stars, and of these the records are in many instances of extraordinary wonderfulness. I must not pause to recount this. I know it very imperfectly.

"My examiners had little to do. My memory seemed of great power, and I told them the story of our experiments, discoveries and our compact to communicate with each other. This portion of my story was listened to with admiration. Chapman, my guide, and the two Registeries leaped to their feet, exclaimed with delight and embraced each other in ecstacy. 'At last! At last!' cried out all of them, while hastily calling officers of the building to them they rapidly explained my singular announcement. It seemed to run like fire through the throngs. A great crowd was soon pressing in upon us on every side, while the Martian ejaculation '*Hi mitla*' rang in all directions. I was astounded. What was this strange excitement, and why had my simple tale awakened this fierce commotion?

"My guide noting my dismay and alarm, laughingly explained the reason of the confusion. 'For years and years,' he said, 'it has been hoped by the Martians to send some message to the Earth. We understand wireless telegraphy, we can bridge almost infinite distances with the monstrous waves of magnetic disturbances, it is possible for us to generate. We have bombarded the earth with magnetic waves, but no response, no single indication has been returned to us that our messages were received. Our knowledge of the earth language is complete, even our knowledge of the telegraphic codes is partially so. But we have hopelessly repeated, are even now repeating these efforts.

"'You, my friend, are the first man from Earth who tells us that wireless telegraphy is understood upon Earth, that receivers have been invented; but above all it amazes and transports us to know that you have perfected means, before leaving the Earth, to have such messages as you may deliver from Mars properly received. There is, though,' he exclaimed, as he turned to the eager, shining faces about me, 'still a grave doubt whether our good friend can assure us of the ability of the *Earthlings* to send us back any communication. They may be unable to force through this enormous distance waves of sufficient magnitude to reach us.'

"There was a loud murmur of disappointment, mingled with exclamations of dissent and reproach. Once more I was plied with questions, and then, my son, there came to me, singularly clouded in forgetfulness until that instant, the memory of that fruitless message which we received about a year before my death on Earth.

"I arose, and amid a hush of expectation excited by this motion, accompanied as it were with a gesture inviting silence, spoke aloud in English:

"'My friends, I recall a night in August, 1890, in the Earth's chronology, when my son and myself, then hoping against hope that the carefully adjusted receiver we had, would ever be called upon to herald a message from another world, were suddenly surprised to see and hear the register of our instrument move and sound. It was indeed animated by some extra terrestrial power. Could that power have come from your Mars; were we the first to receive one of your messages that you have so long been raining on the Earth?'

"I looked around in enthusiasm, and with a conscious sense of companionship, pride and affection. I do not think I was altogether understood, except by a few, but the contagion of my own pleasure seized the multitude, and a great melodious shout arose, while cries of '*Hi mitla*' echoed in the Hall, and then, carried away with an emotional impulse, these excited Martians broke into a song, a swinging chant, that brought to the doors of the room new accessions of spectators whose instantaneous sympathy was expressed by the added volume of sound they contributed, until beneath the vibrant power of the great chorus the building seemed itself to tremble.

"And then a curious and astounding thing happened. My old acquaintance, Chapman, leaped up in the dense clusters, and springing on a table shouted, 'To the Patenta.' The words seemed understood by almost all. I was seized by powerful arms, swung upon the shoulders of two splendid, vigorous youths. While by one impulse the throng surged through the doors in a sort of triumphal progress, I found myself moving in the midst of the excited populace up a broad avenue to the central hill of the city again, which was crowned by the many towers, halls, domes and aggregated arms and facades of the wonderful Patenta, the great communal home of Experiment and Observation.

"The clamor of our approach brought to the scene the dwellers in the houses and the wanderers in the streets. And amongst the great density of forms and faces I saw the phosphorescent figures of many forming spirits swept on in this friendly anarchy of delight and anticipation.

"My son, as I send these words out into the ether-filled realms of space across the millions of miles that intervene between that speck of light on which even now I know you lament my departure, and this new home of mine, which to you also is but a speck of light, I feel in a desperation of doubt that you will never hear them.

"How thrilled and awe-struck I became as I gazed around me, and looking over the surging mob beheld their multitudinous lineaments, the faces of the races of our earth, its many nations, the faces of men or women who had lived in Venus, in Mercury, in the fixed stars, perhaps, as we call those globes from whose lambent surface light reached the earth after the expiration of a century of years. What a beautiful exhilaration of feeling it imparted, these flushed and shining faces, the liquid eyes of the south now charged with the fires of transporting expectation, the steady gaze of blue-eyed northerners firm and rapt and steadfast; the power of huge, colossal frames of muscle, the sinuous activity of spare and slender forms all attired in that consummate garb of blue and white, their caps of metal reflecting the light in cerulean lustres.

"On, upward, we moved, impelled by an impulse quite indefinable but sufficient to condense about us by its contagion the Martian populace, quick, responsive, inquisitive, intelligent and excitable as children. We were approaching the Patenta by an ever widening avenue, our rustling approach announced by a chant of vociferous and yet melodious notes.

"The avenue of Approach is known as the *Imprintum*. On either side rose lines of marble columns, their lofty capitals crowned with statues, their bases clustering with marble groups, while breaking now and then the white monotony, spiral and intertwining pillars of colored glass sprang into the air, like titanic tropical vines holding in extended fingers the balls of phosphori.

"The pavement we trod was made of blocks of the phosphori, and at night this magnificent, indescribable and transcendent street becomes a path of flame, showering upon the files of silent marble statues above it the splendor of this spectral effulgence.

"As we came near the buildings of the Patenta our outcry and the sonorous pulsations of the singing brought to its windows and doorways the many workers in the laboratories, lecture halls, and offices. We were regarded with wonder. But there seems present amongst these people a telepathic power, not perhaps what we call that in the Earth, but an intuitive construction of meaning upon the passing of a word or a hint. Forerunners furthermore had given some account of the strange new spirit from the Earth, who had prearranged with people on the Earth itself, to return to them, if possible, messages of his experiences after a human death. It had been the dream of the Martians, the sensation of their daily lives, the hope of returning to their former dwelling places, some token, word, salutation, indeed to somehow begin that almost apocryphal conception of binding the Universe into a conversational unit.

"No marvel that they were now excited, transported; no wonder that I, the accidental being, who falling in their world, as it were, from outside, should be the agency to lead to the eventual conquest of these great designs.

"On we swept like a tide that advances upon a coast, encompasses each salient rock, island and projection, and evading it by embracing it, rises still further into the bays and harbors, and brings the full tide at last to its most remote limits. So columns and stairways, halls, and wings, and arms, of buildings successively were surged round, and the vast complex pushed its way to the great Hall of Attention.

"This enormous structure was built somewhat to one side of the great Observatories. It was rectangular, elevated and attained to by stairs on every side. It resembles a huge Grecian temple, but the interior treatment was quite contrasted. Externally it was made of the white phosphorescent marble with colonnades of columns of the blue metal supporting its projecting roofs. I was carried as by a cataract of waters up its stairways. Already its bronze gates were swung wide open, and through them the Martian army passed with impetuous stride. Learned men, the leaders and great physicists, many of those I had seen in the morning had reached the Hall. These were constantly augmented by new arrivals from the more distant Schools of Philosophy, Design and Art, while streaming in at every door came the joyous multitude, and the great vault of the Hall of Attention resounded with the rolling chorus.

"It was a moving, an impossible spectacle. The balconies swept upward to a wall of polished granite. They were supported by columns of mosaic marble; the floor of roughened glass was concealed with benches of a gray stone, whose backs were carved in a tracery of branches, over which were thrown pale yellow rugs or shawls; the broad ceiling was divided into deep, rectangular recesses *plafonded* with opalescent glass, and these recesses were made by the intersection of huge girders of the blue metal, while provisions were made throughout for electric lighting by tall glass cylinders, which glow like pillars of lambent flame, and stood upright, affixed to the walls at regular intervals, or concealed in cavities along the ceiling, or grouped like the fasces of the Roman lictors, at the railings of the balconies.

"A wide platform occupied the center of this vast auditorium, and upon this I was carried as by a wave of the sea. Here I touched the floor; the accompanying crowds dispersed through the hall, which became filled, and as it filled some unnoticed signal ushered the glow of the electric ether in the cylinders, until a glory of radiance mingled with the sunlight and illuminated the audience, whose songs had died away, and who sat in attitudes of attention, their faces upturned, their blue caps shining resplendently, like a surface of tempered steel.

"I stood alone with my former guide, and Chapman. I felt moved by some singular enthusiasm; the exaltation of the moment possessed me, and unannounced, as yet unquestioned, I rose to my full height upon a narrow rostrum in the platform, and turning from side to side spoke with an elation that seemed to propel my ringing words over the great assembly with the power and shock of a trumpet:

"'Men and women,' I cried, 'I have reached your wonderful world from that habitation of mortal men known to many of you as the Earth, where death ceaselessly destroys generation after generation, and only the incessant processes of birth as quickly renew the falling ranks of life. To us on earth, the disappearance of those we love and cherish, the sundering of ties which a lifetime of love and companionship has established, the sharp vanishing away into nothingness and silence of the faces and spirits of the great and glorious, the good, the helpful, the true and noble, has made death an awful, hideous, to some a hopeless mystery.

"'We stand on earth speechless before the unseen power which snatches from our caresses all that we most cherish, all that makes our life there worth living. There is no solution of the mystery, no voice, no return, no message, only a blankness of doubt, misgiving and desperate yearning in those who must continue. There is indeed with those on Earth a partial confidence by reason of religious faith, but strong as that seems to be, the endless succession of centuries, each crowding the viewless habitations of the dead with the still more and deeper streams of disembodied souls, unaccompanied by any response, any utterance or return, limit or telltale apparition, has somehow filled all minds with a creeping wonder if even the assurances of Revelation can be believed.

"'Dying on the Earth may have continued in historic, and what is called prehistoric time, for over 50000 years, and yet from those unnumbered millions not a cry or a whisper, note, or vision, is heard or seen to betray their destiny, if destiny beyond the grave there is.

"'But back of Religion, back of experience, back of rational doubt or infidelity, the heart keeps up its importunate cry of hope. We dare not crush out within us the sweet thought of reunion. Upon that earth I lost a wife, who summed up to me everything of value, virtue, and beauty human life can claim. The passionate desire to regain her, the defiant mutiny of my heart against any thought of her annihilation, made me turn to the shining hosts of heaven for reassurance. In them somewhere I believed the vanished soul of my companion had flown. This wonderful world was known to me, and what the wise men of the Earth said of its possible population. It was then that with my son I devised, following certain suggestions, a system of wireless telegraphy. We have both, my son and myself, felt certain that some disturbance was recorded by our instrument from some planet beyond the earth. From that moment my son and myself felt convinced that we might be permitted to bring about a release of the inhabitants of the Earth from the narrow limits of its own surface, and launch out upon the spaces of the universe the messages that would return to us with some news of other worlds, or bring assurance that the Death of the world was but the swinging door to some new existence.

"'Men of Mars, that Death which tore from me my wife set his seal at last on me, but before the summons was executed, I had made arrangements in every possible detail to communicate with my son. We agreed upon a cypher, and I have so imprinted each measure of our compact upon my memory that all of it is as clear to my mind as it was before I left the Earth. Give me possession of your great instruments, let me bridge the millions of miles to our earth, and in an instant stir the populations of the Earth into fierce attention, so that from now on through all the coming years you Martians shall speak with the people of the earth and again from Mars, as from some relay station, messages shall pass outward to the stars, and thus from planet to planet the reinforced utterance may pierce the universe of worlds.'

"I finished; a great shout arose from the immense multitude; with one impulse the light blue metal caps were swung from their heads and tossed upward, while the cheers passing out into the streets were caught up, and in refluent waves of sound rolled back upon me like the murmur of a distant storm at sea.

"I do not think I was quite understood, but the chief feature of my speech was realized, and the Martians, quick to respond to any suggestion, and inflammable of nature, had become enthusiastic over the prospects of this new revelation.

"I stood an instant uncertain what I should do, or what new development would follow my evident popularity. Suddenly a strong, ringing voice spoke from the gallery immediately in front of me. It said—I could not quite separate the speaker in the moving throng: 'Come to the *Manana*.'

"Chapman and my friend whispered together 'Volta,' and then turning to me told me to follow them. I followed. Already the hall had become partially emptied, and we pushed onward amongst radiant men and women, who received me with smiles and gestures of approval. Once outside the Hall of Attention, we hurried through some narrow corridors, up winding stairways, until at length we emerged upon a lofty platform carrying a railing about it, and so elevated above all the surrounding buildings of the Patenta that my glance seemed to sweep the circuit of the City, and swept outward over a rolling and low country through which ran wide mirror-like ribbons of water, the great canals of Mars, while afar off melting into the crystalline hazes of the horizon rose dark masses of mountains.

"I stood an instant stupified and overcome. The deep voice of a salutation came to my ears, and turning I saw the face of Volta. Beside me was a large induction coil, and above it two huge plates of copper about ten feet apart. The next instant a flash passed between the electrodes, and I was caught and turned aside with my companions. The light of the spark was intense, and the spark itself of great dimensions.

"Volta then spoke: 'My friend, your arrival on the surface of our planet is a sensation. We are all delighted. You have solved our difficulties. With this transmitter you can yourself send to the earth the message you wish. And this receiver will catch the waves of the smallest amplitudes.'

"He pointed to a singular train of tubes, each filled apparently with a shining line of straw shaped metallic bodies. This was raised by some silk cord passing to a pulley and arm, perhaps a hundred feet above us.

"Volta spoke with difficulty; he seemed preoccupied, and after I was shown the transmitter, and its mechanism was explained, he took my hand warmly, pressed it between his own, and then speaking in the Martian tongue to Chapman, left us.

"I then sent you, my son, my first message. What pleasure! The great sparks flashed magnificently. Chapman and my friend were in ecstacies. I worked steadily until the night. And when all was over I waited until the stars came out, until again the City of Light shone like some huge, myriad faceted stone, and then there came, while Chapman and my friend stood mute beside me, your faint response.

"I scarcely caught the lisping ticks, but they came, and it seemed indeed as if the power of the Creator had passed into the hands of men.

"With a joy too deep for the futile hopelessness of words to express, we both descended from the high station and through the great halls. I found my way to the charming, peaceful room above the glowing city and fell asleep with prayers upon my lips for all the dead and dying upon the Earth.

"The next day as I awoke I found my friend and Chapman waiting for me. I felt wonderfully refreshed, and the exultant mood of the Martians possessed me. I sang with an interior tumult of excitement. I drew before my mind the beauty of your mother reincorporated in this gay, lovely world of Mars, so full of power and light and youthful impulse. Again I sang, and it was the very air your mother so often played to me, 'Der Grüne Lauterband,' of Schubert. A few passers by, below my window, caught the refrain, my voice rose higher and higher, and their disappearing figures seemed to carry the merry, hopping notes far away. How fair and glorious it all was!

"And I was to visit Scandor, to visit the beautiful Martian country, the mines, the huge fossil ivory deposits, to sail on those canals, whose resplendent lines we had detected from the earth.

"My door was shaken, and almost as if yet living on the earth, I cried out 'Come in.' Chapman and my friend entered with laughter and congratulation. Chapman spoke first: 'Dodd, you are summoned to the Council of the Patenta. All are anxious to see you. At present it is hoped you will not push further the matter of the telegraphy with the Earth. The disturbances in Pike increase daily—flashing stars seem to emerge from nothing, meteoric showers, like a rain of sparks rush across the fields of the telescopes, gaseous disengagements from what seem like shining nuclei, shoot upward for thousands of miles from their surfaces; all is chaos, and these disturbances have been noticed in other regions of the heavens. Again spirits have ceased arriving at the Hill of the Phosphori, the Chorus Halls are almost empty, and the singers have no employment. Such a dearth of spirits has not been known before for months. It is not uncommon for long intervals to occur when only a few spirits arrive, but now there are none.

"'The Registeries report that many lately reincarnated spirits speak the languages of Venus and Mercury, and tell of the terrific physical convulsions in both planets, that wars are raging in Mercury, and a singular plague devastating Venus. The country people have sent in word by the canals that rockets in clusters covering hundreds of square miles are arising from Scandor. The cause is unknown, cannot even be surmised, and last night Herschell and Gauss, at the big telescopes, detected a comet charging towards us with an incredible velocity. The Council believe I should at once start for Scandor to bring the month's report, and these new excitements, to the paper Dia, while they urge that you should recount to the governors at Scandor your story, and the marvellous fact of the answer sent back from the Earth to you by your son. We will go, after an audience with the Council, together, and because of some need of more stone from the quarries, we will stop on our way out and leave orders at Mit and Sinsi, where the quarries are. The trip is full of beauty and wonder, and Scandor, I am told, is Heaven itself.'

"He paused. I thought there was a shade of disappointment in my friend's face, as Chapman drew me to one side, and I stepped quickly back to him, and said: 'Will you not go with us, too? You first cared for me and brought me food and raiment.' His eyes were again bright with peace. 'No, my new friend, I cannot go now. I am waiting, waiting here at the City of Light, watching the spirits, if perchance my son from your earth is amongst them. Surely he will come some day, and then my happiness will be all God can make it.'

"We hurried away to the Chamber of the Council. Once more through the devious paths of the great groups of buildings which make up the

Patenta, between the flowering trees and the tulip flowered vines we made our way, with feet so buoyant and so strong that we seemed almost to fly.

"The Chamber of the Council of the Patenta was a beautiful room. It was one of the few great chambers in the City of Light, dressed in color and tapestries. A deep carpet of scarlet Talta wool covered the floor, and there hung at irregular intervals from a silver cornice deep green curtains. The furniture was very wonderful. A dark wood, like teak, opulently fitted with silver, formed the great table that occupied the center of the room, as also the heavy chairs on which were placed cushions of a golden yellow silk. There were no windows in the room. The light entered from above through two simple round apertures covered with white glass. Book cases stood about the room filled with large folios, which, as I observed from a few spread upon the table, were not printed books, but filled with writing in a round, clear hand, legible at some distance.

"But the most extraordinary feature of the room was a marvellous colossal figure at one end of the room, in a recess richly hung with green tapestries. It was cast in silver upon which dull shades and frosted and polished surfaces were appropriately combined, as their position required, in the portrayal of a Being of incredible benignity of expression, attired in flowing robes with an outstretched hand, his face invested with a harmonious union of power and sweetness. Beneath it upon the enormous black pedestal the letters in silver were conspicuous—Tarunta—the Deity. This amazing creation arrested the attention of my friend Chapman, and myself, and we stood half spell-bound under the influence of its seraphic and potent beauty.

"The next moment we were conscious of the throng filling the room. There were many of the great physicists and chemists and astronomers and observers whom I had seen at the breakfast in the Dining Hall the previous morning with a few others who were the first men I had seen in Mars wearing the expression of age. They almost seemed venerable. I remembered then what I had learned on my arrival at the Patenta—that age and death also supervene in Mars.

"I was observed at once, and friendly hands were extended to me from all sides. I was led to the head of the table. There I was invited to enlarge my story as given in the Hall of Attention, and I was told to tell it in English. A scribe near me conveyed to pads of paper my narrative.

"When I had finished an audible murmur of approval filled the room, and the most aged of the older men arising, and speaking in Martian, translated to me by the scribe, said:

"'My friend, you have delighted us. The time is approaching when we can, I trust, receive such visitors from all the worlds, and gradually bring it to pass that the visible universe may be bound together through the power and sympathy of language. The Council desires that at present you refrain from sending your second message until you have visited Scandor, and seen something of this new world upon which you have so auspiciously alighted.

"'Heroma (Sir, Sire, etc., etc.), Chapman will accompany you. The government at Scandor should be apprized of certain strange celestial conditions, and we are in receipt of news that at Scandor also unusual things are happening. While all we know or have observed could be transmitted to Scandor, and all their own knowledge in turn sent to us by wireless telegraphy, for reasons which we are not at liberty to explain at present, it has been thought best to send the approved diary of the Patenta to the government, and also learn in return, by word of mouth, what has transpired at our capital. It will afford you some opportunity to visit the Martian Mountains, and be more informed for the second message you are expected to transmit to the Earth when you return.'

"After a few salutations, in which interview I found myself face to face with the reincarnated forms of some of the greatest scientific thinkers who have lived upon our globe, I left the Council Chamber with my friend and Chapman, to prepare for our coming journey. It was then that I entered more deeply the City of Light, and saw the unspeakable splendor of the Garden of the Fountains.

"The Garden of the Fountains lies over toward the great Halls of Philosophy, Design and Invention, whose domes and temple-pointed roofs of copper and blue metal I could easily discern. It covers over half a square mile of space. It is supplied with water from an enormous lake resting in the hollow of an extinct volcano, fifty miles to the east of the City of Light, at an elevation of 5,000 feet. A great conduit or water main, as we would say, conveys the water to the garden. The Garden is built actually upon piers of concrete and stone, connected by arches of brick, and through the subterranean chambers, thus formed, the division of the streams is made, and there controlled. The whole was designed by the great Martian artist, Hinudi, whom some aver is the reincarnated Leonardo da Vinci of our Earth.

"The Garden is approached through a labyrinthine avenue made up of Palms, which on that side of the City seem to be plentiful, and over these palms in extraordinary profusion the vines of the red flowered honeysuckle. You cannot see beyond the wall of green on either side in this winding way, and only as you gaze upward does the eye escape the imprisonment of its surroundings, where above the waving summits of the palms you see a lane of the bluest sky.

"As you draw near the debouchment (into the garden) of this oscillating road, the splash and roar of falling waters invades your retreat. And then suddenly as if a curtain had arisen or dropped to the earth you emerge upon a great marble terrace of steps, and before you is spread a forest of geysers distributed in entrancing vistas in a lake of tumbling and scintillating waters. The scene is amazing and transporting. Rushing jets of water are enclosed in hollow pillars of glass, whose lines are ravishingly combined in the separate clusters of fountains.

"The heights of these fountains vary from 150 to 200 feet, and they are arranged in a peculiar disorder, which, however, conforms to an elaborate plan. The water rises in these colored tubes in green columns, then breaks into sheets and bubble-laden cataracts of spray above them, pouring far outward like blazing showers of little lamps in the full sunlight. Many of the tubes are inclined, and the ejected shafts of water collide above them, producing explosive clouds of shattered vesicles of moisture that float off or drop in miniature rains over the lake. This wildness of fountains extends over many a mile. All the jets are not in tubes. Many uncovered fountains are interjected amongst the glass pillars.

"The pillars vary in form, and have much diversity of aperture, so that the water shoots from them in every posture and form. It makes a bewildering picture. The exposure of water in the great lake or pond which holds these fountains is broken with waves, and the tempestuous scene with the constant excitement of the rising and flowing avalanches of water creates feelings of abounding wonder. The marble steps extend around the lake, and behind them on all sides rises the wall of the palms, beaten into motion by the wind blowing ceaselessly. The esplanade-like margin between the top step and the palm enclosure accommodated great numbers, while the benches in retreating alcoves, were also filled.

"It was a varied, exhilarating scene. The moving throngs, the wonderful confusion of the spouting fountains in their chrysalids of glass against the sky line, the perpetually waving fronds of the palms!

"We hurried to the pier of the Registeries after Chapman had secured the sealed envelope, in which were placed the communications to the government at Scandor. The canal which enters the City of Light at this point is divided into a number of branches whose confluent arms, about a mile from the City, unite into two parallel canals whose course we were now to follow to the City of Scandor. The small boat we entered was a curious vessel of white porcelain, broad and short, with raised keel, prow, and expanded stern.

"It was moved by some motor, electric in nature. A pilot took his place at the bow, and, under a canopy of silk, in the light of a setting sun, followed by the music of the City, we passed away from the City, which, even as we left it, slowly, in the descending darkness of the night, began to kindle into light, and send upward into the velvet zenith its phosphorescent glows."

CHAPTER V

"It was afternoon when Chapman and I, fully equipped and provisioned, moved off from the long granite pier at the Registeries, after an affectionate parting from my guide and friend, who returned sorrowfully to resume his watch for his son, whose coming to Mars seemed to him so assured.

"How wonderfully strange and exciting it all seemed! Down the crowded canal we slowly moved, amidst the calling crews, the pleasant cheers, and beckonings of sightseers; and back of us rose on its hills the City of Light, that, as we passed still further away, and watched it in the fading sunset, began to glow, and finally, to shine like some titanic opal in the velvet shadows of the night.

"These numerous arms of the canal some miles from the City coalesce and merge into the enormous trunk canal that passes on to Scandor through hills and mountains and the plain country, excavated by the wonderful Toto powder. This trunk canal is doubled; upon one member, the boats pass outward to Scandor, and on the other the boats return. Branches pass north and south at centers of population, and of some of these which pass actually into the frozen depths of the polar countries, I may tell you later.

"As we slowly progressed into the undulating plain country, with its villages and farm lands, diversified by woods, and sometimes solitary projections of rock, as the stars stole urgently into the sky, as the phosphori lamps began their soft illumination of the decks, and while murmurs of songs from merrymakers on the land came to us in snatches bewitchingly, though incongruously mingled with the delicious odors of the Napi grass, I turned to Chapman, and felt that now, throughout the hours of the genial night, I would pour out unchecked the flood of inquiry that had risen again and again to my lips in this strange new life.

"'Chapman,' I began, 'you must feel that I have a great deal to ask you. This new life, with its surprises and the strange incidents of the two or three days I have already lived here have suggested so many questions, can we not now talk about these marvels?'

"'Certainly,' replied Chapman, as he lifted a glass of delicate pearl pink, filled with the pungent and keenly stimulating *Ridinda*, to his lips. 'Put on your thinking cap, and perforate me with all the puzzles you can think of. I am a trifle rattled myself in this new ranch—have not been here long—but I tell you, Dodd, Mars is first class. It suits me. Never enjoyed living so much, never found it so much a matter of course, and as to livelihood, when I think of those freezing nights on the earth in Rutherford's cheesebox shooting at the moon with wet plates, I can tell you this sort of thing isn't a long call from all I ever hoped to find in Heaven. Open your batteries. To-morrow will be full of sight-seeing, and I guess you will forget all you want to know to-day in trying to remember what you will see then.' He took another sip of the snapping liquid, drew his chair closer to my own, and while a sort of musical echo lingered in the air, I began:

"'Chapman, where on Mars are we? I seem to feel neither heat nor cold. I see these flowers, the palms in the Garden of the Fountains, day passes into night, and there is no very apparent change of temperature, so far as feeling goes. What are we made of? Is this new body we carry insensible to heat or cold? I feel indeed my pulse beat. I am conscious of warmth in the sun, and of coolness in the shade. I feel the wind blow on my cheeks, but all these sensations are so much less keen than on the earth, and yet again I realize that sensations are in some ways as vivid as on the earth. The pleasure of my ears and eyes is wonderfully deep and exhaustive, the sense of taste rapid and delightful. I am happy, supremely happy, and affection, even the hidden fires of love, burn in my veins as on the earth.' Chapman looked at me with that bright smile he wore on earth, and his gestures of expostulation were amusing. 'Wait, Dodd, don't talk so fast. You remember I had a slow way on the earth. I have no reason to think it will prove any less pleasant to stay slow on Mars. One thing at a time. My own sense of position is not so secure that I can tell exactly all you want to know, and there are a good many things that the heavyweights up here don't pretend yet to explain. Now, where are we? Well, the City of Light is about 40 degrees south of the Martian equator, not so far from what on earth would be the position of Christ Church, where you "shuffled off the mortal coil." Don't frown. Mars is a serene, sweet place, but I am not yet so intimidated by the lofty life here as to drop my jokes. Some Martians strike me as a trifle heavy in style, just a suggestion of a kind of sublimated Bostonese about them, don't you know. Curious! However, the ordinary Martian is gamy, good company, full of happiness, with a considerable fancy for jokes, absurdly addicted to music, and as credulous as a child. Somehow, Dodd, a good deal of my earthly nature has stuck to me, and I revel in a dual life. I have my Martian side, but I can't, and this life can't, knock the old foibles of the world you left, out of me yet. I may get the proper sort of exultation in time, but just now I've imported considerable human horse sense.'

"He looked at me whimsically; I walked away, and watched the receding city.

"The motion of our white boat was so smoothly rapid, that soon, and almost unnoticed we had threaded all the many lanes, windings, and locks that led to the broad canals some twenty miles from the city. We had passed laden barges, flat and storied boats carrying excursions or freight, and trains of smaller craft crowded with fruit brought in from distant farms for the great population of the City of Light. The scene assumed a fairy-like unreality as night settled down, and the boats swarming with light, or else carrying a few red lanterns, passed us while their occupants or owners chanted the lonely lullaby of the Martians, which begins: 'Ana cal tantil to ti.'

"It was yet to me all a wonderful dream, from which each moment I dreaded awakening. It was all so beautiful!

"I sat again with Chapman under the canopy, talking of the earth. Strange Mystery! Here we were with our earth memories yet vivid, recalling incidents of life in New York City, and summoning amid all the appealing charm of this strange new life, the little, sordid variances and trials, vexations and minor sufferings that had marred his own life on earth. We turned to these things, not because they were grateful or pleasing to remember, but because it seemed to *establish* us, or rather me, to give me identity, and build up the growing certainty that I had come from the earth, and was re-embodied in this new sphere of active feeling and experience.

"I told him of you, of the death of your mother, of our flight to New Zealand, our experiments, the Dodans, and then turning to him, as we saw the Martian moon rise in ruddy fullness far away over the hill of *Tiniti*, I said, searchingly: 'Chapman, you remember Martha? How beautiful and good she was! I have kept one long, sad, and still deathless hope in my repining heart. I shall see her again! It must be! I have felt so certain of this that no argument, no appeal to reason, can drive away the keen sense of its realization. Have you seen her on Mars amongst the thousands you have met, and is there on this entrancing orb any other place than the Hill of the Phosphori, for the disembodied of other worlds to enter this new world?

"Chapman smiled. 'Yes,' he answered, 'I remember your wife very well. I could pick her out from ten thousand, but I have never seen her yet in the City of Light. You may, my dear friend, cherish only an illusion, and yet I am half willing to agree with you; such intuitive feelings have a deeper philosophy of truth than we can fathom, and no laughing skepticism, no mere frivolous doubt can expel them. Wait, my friend; it may yet be meant for you to meet her. And now I do recall some accounts told me of occasional visitants to Mars entering its life at different points; many indeed have been received near Scandor, and on one or two occasions the prehistoric peoples, the little strong men of the mountains and the northern ice have brought in such a chance waif that has become body amongst them. How wild and frightened they become! And quite naturally! Ghosts dropping out of the air becoming flesh and blood might startle a rational being into a rigid course of religious practices, not to say superstition. But look, how fair the night has become.'

"The landscape about us was wonderfully illuminated by the two satellites, Deimos and Phobos, which, as you well know, were made known to astronomers on the earth by Prof. Asaph Hall in 1877. What a marvellous spectacle they presented, moving almost sensibly at their differing rates of revolution through a sky sown with stellar lights. The combined lights of these singular bodies surpassed the light of our terrestrial moon, by reason of their closeness to the surface of Mars, while the more rapid motion of the inner satellite causes the most weird and beautiful changes of effect in the nocturnal glory they both lend to the Martian life.

"We were sailing in a broad river-like canal, perhaps one mile or more wide. On all sides the undulating ground, covered with cultivation, varied with thick patches of trees, with here and there shining lights from villages and isolated homes, carried the eye onward to a rising hill country, beyond which, again, silhouetted against the shining sky where Phobos began to rise mountain tops were just discernible.

"Deimos, the outer moon, was already shining, and its pale, sick light imparted a peculiar blueness impossible to describe upon all surfaces it touched. Here was the phenomenon we witnessed with increasing pleasure. Phobos was emerging from a cloud and its yellow rays possessing a greater illuminating power, mingled suddenly with the blue and spectral beams of Deimos and the land thus visited by the complimentary flood of light from these twin luminaries seemed suddenly dipped in silver. A beautiful white light, most unreal, as you mortals might say, fell on tree and water, cliff, hill, and villages. The effect was not unlike that instant in photography when a developing plate shows the outlines of its objects in dazzling silver before the half tints are added, and the image fades away into indistinguishable shadow.

"It was a print in silver, and while we gazed in mute astonishment the sharp shadows changed their position as Phobos, racing through the zenith, changed the inclination of its incident beams. The effect was indescribable. I walked the deck in an agitation of wonder and delight. Chapman, to whom the novelties of this Martian life were still wonderful, followed me, and was the first to speak.

"'Dodd, you know that the strangest thing about this whole place is your body. It's body all right enough, but I can't quite understand what sort of a body it is. It hurts in a way, and is pleased in a way, but it seems a better made affair in texture and parts than anything we possessed on earth. Exertion is so easy.'

"'Well, Chapman,' I answered, while my eyes rested on the water, through which an approaching barge rose like a vessel of frosted or burnished white metal, 'we were taught on the earth that, with gravitation reduced one-half, the same weight on Mars would seem only half as heavy as on the earth, and that the effort which there carried us eight feet would here send us sixteen.'

"'It is true,' returned Chapman, 'but that doesn't explain everything. We sleep less here, we scarcely touch meat, and yet exertion, prolonged by hours, scarcely accelerates the blood or vexes the nerves, and generally we don't grow old. Our bodies are light; the texture, apparently firm and resisting, is somehow diaphanous. I've seen the light through the palm of my hand. And then again I haven't. Somehow mind works in the body here and changes it, and changes it different at different times. Why, Dodd, the other day at the Patenta, a student jumped up with a cry of delight at something, and stumbled and fell from a window to the ground, but he stood up without a bruise or hurt of any kind. His exultation, his emotional excitement made him buoyant, I think, and he fell to the earth like a thistledown. There was no concussion.'

"'Well,' I responded, 'I cannot tell. I know very little as yet. I feel wonderfully active and vitalized. My senses are acute. I see further, hear further, smell further than I ever did on earth, and it even seems to me I can anticipate things. The nerve currents are so rapid, the mind seems so persuasive, that coming events are registered by a prophetic feeling I can scarcely describe. For that reason, Chapman, I grow happier every minute, for now I see approaching that great joy, my reunion with Martha, the one great divine event I hunger and hope for.

"'Well,' said Chapman, as a cloud covered the scudding moons, 'I do hope you may see her, and somehow I think, too, you will. But, Dodd,' the moons emerged, and the lower one was in transit across the face of the upper, 'I must call your attention to this strange peculiarity of our bodies, that we undergo extremes of temperature with almost no noticeable sense of the great heat or cold. This region we are traversing is about the latitude of Christ Church, as I told you, and it is the period of harvests, and the heat is moderate, but in the height of summer the heat seems scarcely more felt than now, and in the clothing I am now wearing, I have sailed through the ice packs of the North, and slept thinly covered in its snows, but without undue discomfort. I tell you, matter in us, and flesh and blood in us are all differently conditioned.'

"'Why not ask these questions of the wise men of the Patenta, the doctors and chemists?' I replied. 'I can think of an analogy that might make this Martian constitution intelligible. A close, dense body conducts heat or cold; a loose, open texture or cellular mass does not. In our curious embodiment from spirit the substance of our bodies is an etherealized matter, loosely, I might say, flocculently, disposed, and while it conveys sensations of a certain tone or key of vibratory intensity, it will not respond to any violent or coarse shocks. They simply cannot be carried. They escape us. Are the people all alike amongst the Martians?'

"'Oh, no,' returned Chapman, who pointed to the widening spaces in the beams between the slow Deimos and the fleeter flying Phobos, 'there are great differences. I have seen that. In materialization some seem badly put together, and these resemble our former terrestrial bodies. They grow old, they succumb to disease, they feel changes of weather and they have less vitality. Yes,' and he drew nearer, 'it is these unhappy misbirths in this spirit land who retain the sin of earth and cannot survive and get the *Kinkotantitomi* or irreverently, as the earthling would say, the grand bounce. They are fired off the planet.'

"He paused and laughed. How strange this almost human laugh sounded, and yet how pleasant! I looked at him with a deep affection. He noticed the impression, and quickly drawing me to him, said half timidly:

"'Dodd, that sort of laugh and those words of mine just used, are not Martian, they don't belong to these rarefied beings here. They have a human or earthly taint, and they frighten me. I seem so lonely sometimes. My stray fun which I once enjoyed on earth must somehow be forgotten here. I feel so irreverent at times, so full of horse play, but I must keep up the high key and act like the rest. Indeed for the most of the time I feel as they do, I suppose, but sometimes that sort of ribaldry and feelings of the ludicrous that made us joke, and prank, and cut up in genial companionships come over me, and I am suffocating with a glee out of place to this exalted society. Ah! it's good to feel you, my friend, so fresh and new from earth. It's promised here in the learned talk I have heard, that those who disappear from Mars become reincorporated upon earth again, if they belong there. Well, I wouldn't mind if I got returned, wonderful and sweet and happy as all this seems. The dear, dear old Earth!'

"He flung his arms around me, and our faces met, as if we had been lost brothers. A sort of terrifying melancholy invaded me. I was so distant from all I had known and loved, so distant from the surges we had watched from our observatory at Christ Church, so distant from the life of heat and clothing and genial domesticities; the life even, it might be called, of the daily paper, the novel, the new book, the life of politics and human history, and conventionality, the life of ups and downs, of sickness and health, of individual enterprise, of routine and mechanical fatigue, the life of exertion, contrast and social inequality, with its picturesqueness, its incessant interest, all this was now utterly removed by all the measureless leagues of icy space between me and the floating planet—the old sin-stricken Earth—that was shining in the Martian skies, so inconspicuous and tiny—so inaccessible.

"But my heart was pulsating audibly. If I could recover Martha, if, in this serene atmosphere of good will and fairness and kindness, in the midst of unknown possibilities of knowledge, in the company of enthusiastic and high-minded men and women, in this arena of scientific wonders, and in the joy and beauty of universal happiness and thrift and peace and well doing and intuition, I could find a human companionship in the woman whose face and nature have summed up for me the whole of life, if I could find her! then, indeed, this new world would be all my earthly home could be, and the endless future with her for guide and friend would lose its terror and lonely isolation, and—I dared to think it—even the presence of God himself become bearable.

"Chapman had stolen away from me. He had stolen to the little, dainty rooms that were sunk in the cockpit or cabin of our boat, and I was standing alone in the light of the midnight moons in Mars, a waif from the far earth, incomprehensibly born after death into this human presentiment and renewal in youth, and again instinct with revivified passion and desire; and breathing the atmosphere of a planet that for years I had watched through the tube of a telescope, as a floating flake of celestial fire. A delicious drowsiness overcame me, and while I noticed the pilot was changed, his place being taken by another, and that we were approaching a ridgy or disturbed country, I found my way to the white couch prepared for me, and sank into a deep and dreamless sleep.

"The morning of the next day was clear and beautiful. Shall I ever forget that first approach to the mountains of Tiniti, where Mit and Sinsi, the villages of the quarries, are located. All day long the boat propelled through a diversified country, covered with morainal heaps—great hills of drift matter, heaps of worn pebbles and rolling plains of estuarine sediment. Much of this land seemed untouched with cultivation, and sublime forests of the loftiest trees covered it. The canal passed through solitudes, where the silence was only broken by the cackling laugh of a crane-like bird, marching in lines along the banks, or perched like sleepy sentinels amid the outstretched branches of the trees.

"These wild and fascinating regions were often alternated by miles of bright plantations radiant with the yellow leaves of the Rint, bearing its deep red pods, while avenues of palms, not unlike the royal palm of the

Earth, led in long vistas to clustering groups of houses, and we, too, caught glimpses of basking lakes on which, even as in the Earth, the patient fisherman in basket-like circular boats, waited for his flashing captives.

"Then, again, there were prairie-like stretches of a sort of pampas waving in cloudy lines, the glistening pappus of the wild Nitoti, a peculiar, low composite, that grows in abundance and furnishes food to the strange gazelle of this latitude in Mars.

"This animal, the Rimondi, could be seen in scampering herds over these plains, its horns making an hour glass form above its head, as they bent to each other, touched, and then curved outward again to reunite a second time.

"We were rapidly moving northward, and just as it would be on the earth, the changing vegetation gave visible notice of our advance.

"But more interesting than nature were the scenes of life along our way, and the custom of public worship filled me with wonder. Amphitheatres of stone built high above the ground, and approached by encircling terraces of steps dotted the country at long intervals. These, Chapman explained, were the churches of the people. Here they gathered from long distances around, and, even as he described their meaning, the congregations were seen assembling, while later we heard the music flung in waves of sound from these houses of song and worship.

"Chapman did not understand the Martian faith. There seemed little to understand about it. It was one national expression of the love of goodness and of beauty, but it was all directed to a source of infallible wisdom, power and justice.

"Thus considering the country and its customs we fell again into a long colloquy:

"'Dodd,' said Chapman, musingly, 'we should all become as these people about us, and do the same things, and believe and act as they do. You will, but I think I remain a little strange. I seem a spectator that a caprice has cast upon this globe, and though I live here, I must succumb to a certain alienation, a lack of mediation between their life and my former existence, and because of this subtle estrangement, I shall contract disease, or meet with accident, or waste in age, while you shall stay young, and living, sink into the Martian life and yield to it a spiritual, a mental acquiescence. You will become absorbed, and, with your love realized, the whole rhapsodic life of this world will mingle you forever in its tide of song and science and labor.'

"'Yes,' I answered, 'I am sure I shall. For whatever period of time I stay here, I am one with this beautiful and strange life. I respond naturally to all this serenity and joy, this precision of power over inanimate things; this flooded being and the dawning sense that through the stepping stone of Mars, I approach yet higher beatitudes of living. At least in Mars the sordid taint of suffering, of ignominious physical torture and privation, which spoiled the Earth, is almost unknown.'

"Chapman laughed, and an echo gave back from some hillside its musical response. 'Ah, it may be, I know it is true, and yet—and yet—the Earth possessed a pictorial, a dramatic power in its contrasts of happiness and suffering, of goodness and sin. It had literary material. Its consecutive growth in the ages of social and national and economic history were so wonderful, so thrilling in interest, in the details of character and adventure, in the incessant panoramic display it gave of light and shade. And on it rested the shadow of a strange, pathetic doubt, the mystery of creation. Its romance, its fiction, its fable, and the animating picture it furnished, with its sceptics and its believers, its haters and its lovers, its tyrants and its heroes. Its wide, verbal immensity! I miss all that, or almost all. This life is evenly celestial, and glowing, and carelessly happy. And here knowledge is extreme and pervasive and omnipotent. The dear commonplaces of the Earth life are unknown too, the ludicrous is absent, and the sublimity of sacrifice impossible.'

"He laughed again, and I felt for one brief, incredible instant a pang, too, that the blossoming, full, sensual Earth has passed from beneath my feet forever.

"But it was past. For me nothing was left behind when Martha had gone before. The future for me was the pilgrimage through worlds for her lost face. The sum and substance of a world's growth, of the unintermittent and heraldic progress of the soul was union with her. And deeper in my convictions than science or faith or desire, lay the consciousness of my sure approach.

"Again the evening fell. We arrived at the entrance of a gloomy and stupendous gorge. It was the wonderful passage driven through the first area of igneous rocks before we reached the quarry country of the Tiniti. It pierced the dark and stubborn dike that rose in sheer walls like the Palisades on the Hudson, 1,000 and 1,200 feet above our heads, and it seemed that the darkening tide was carrying us into the bowels of the sphere. As the precipitous walls rose on either side, a loud report, followed by another more muffled, startled us. Looking upward, Chapman, shouting '*Golki, tanto,*' with outstretched hand pointed to a flaming missile passing over our heads, and apparently in the direction we were heading.

"It was a meteor. It was just such a phenomenon as we know of on the Earth. I felt certain that it was a bolide from space, one of those fiery visitors of stone and iron that collide occasionally with our Earth, and that somewhere before us, in the country we were approaching, it would be found.

"Later a few straggling shooting stars appeared. The languor of fatigue overcame me, and I slept prostrate on the cushions of the deck as the murmurous reverberations from the walls of the rock-bound canal rose and fell, with the cadence of the waves, splashing softly against their feet.

"I dreamt of the Earth, the pictures naturally recalled, by these surroundings, of my life on the Hudson River in New York, and it seemed so real, that I should find myself with you working away in the old laboratory at Yonkers near the Albany Road. Suddenly I was shaken, and opening my eyes I beheld the firmament of heaven falling in coruscating cascades about us. Starting up, I found myself clutching Chapman, who had called to the pilot to stop the boat. A few of the attendants were grouped near us, and the loudly suppressed exclamations made me realize that these visitations were perhaps infrequent upon Mars.

"It was a meteoric shower, like our leonids in November. It rained pellets or balls of fire, these phosphorescent trains gleaming spectrally, while a kind of half audible crackling accompanied the fall. Shooting in irregular shoals or volleys, they would increase and diminish, and recurrent explosions announced the arrival at the ground of some meteoric mass.

"It was a marvellous and splendid scene. It lasted till the dawn. We remained almost unchanged in position, while the tiny comets crowded the sky with their uninterrupted march, and the air was shot through with intermingled lanes of light.

"As the morning broke, we had passed the great gorge in the canal, and had entered a wild, savage, almost treeless country. Great weathered columns of rock stood alone in the debris of their own dismemberment, the bare gray or rusty and jagged expanses sloping up steeply from the edge of the canal, sparingly dotted over with gray bushes, and covered with an ashen colored lichen.

"The scene was here forbidding and desolate. We moved for miles through the waste of a ruined world. The whole region had been the stage of great volcanic activity, and the monticules of scoriaceous rock, the broad plains excavated with deep pools that reflected their dismal, untenanted borders in the black depths of unruffled water, spoke of meteorological conditions long prolonged and intense. It was a weird, strange place, silent and dead. But amongst these vast ejections, these truncated fossil craters were embedded masses of the rare self-luminous stone that made the City of Light. Chapman told me how in pockets or huge amygdaloidal cavities, this white phosphorescent substance was quarried, brought up bodily perhaps in the slow upheaval of the region from the deep-seated sources of this mineral flood.

"The canal passed along for miles in the depression between two folds of the surface. Finally, gazing ahead, there slowly came into view a huge *rictus*, a gaping rent in the side of the black and gray and red walls to our right, and a minute movement of living forms, scarcely discernible, revealed the first quarry near the little town of Sinsi.

"As we drew nearer I descried a slant incline from the open excavation down which the blocks of stone were slid. They were brought to the surface by hoisting cranes, and just as our little porcelain cockle-shell glided to the dock, an enormous fragment rudely shaped into a cubical form, was moving down the metal road bed to the edge of the canal.

"Here we landed, and a crowd of people hailed us, and amongst them were many of the prehistoric people, the short, sturdy brown or copper colored northerners who work in the quarries and mines. It was nightfall. Their day's work was over, and they crowded around us with interest. They were good-natured, but quiet, and dressed in a kind of overalls that was made in one garment from head to feet.

"Chapman pushed amongst them, followed by me. We made our way to a pleasant house, built of the quarried volcanic rock, alternating with the white stone of the quarry, and covered with an almost flat roof of the blue metal. In this house we were received by the Superintendent of Quarries, a supernatural, who still retained a mechanical aptitude, brought with him from the earth. The greetings were pleasant, and as the Superintendent spoke his former earth language, which had been French, we got along intelligibly.

"The rooms of this house were large, square apartments, simply furnished with the white chairs, tables and couches I had seen in the City of Light, but on its walls were drawings and photographs of the quarry, the country, and groups of the workmen. Amongst the pictures were some wonderful large scenes of an ice country, and the lustrous high wall of a gigantic glacier. I pointed these out to Chapman. He told me that to the north of the mountains lay the great northern sea, in winter a sea of ice, and that from continental elevations within it glacial masses pushed outward, invading the southern country. A road led over the mountain from Sinsi to regions beyond, where there were fertile intervals and plains inhabited by populations of the small, early people we had met.

"Here were their settlements, from which the workmen of the quarries had been brought. Beyond this again lay the margins of the polar sea. The Superintendent—his name was Alca—had visited this region, and probably made the pictures I wondered at. The Superintendent said we should visit the great quarry in the morning before we started again for Scandor. And he showed us, as the darkness descended about us, a marvellous phenomenon. Standing on the roof of his house, we looked up the mountain side to the immense opening forced in its flank, and it had become a great surface of palpitating, rising and falling light. The waves of glorious soft radiance bathed the village about us, the waters of the canal, and the arid crusts of rock beyond, the circle of encompassing darkness straining like a great black wall, on its spent edges.

"Song and music closed the day, and after eating the wine-soaked cakes of Pintu, we made our way to the white and simple bedchamber and waited for the morning.

"It came, fresh and splendid. The air of this latitude of Mars is so pure, vivid and dustless! My strength and power and vitality seemed boundless. And as in the broad mirror of my bedchamber I viewed my reflection, I leaped with wonder to see the youth I had been, formed anew in lineaments, fairer than Earth's. My son, I have become younger than yourself, age has vanished, and all the restraint of differing years between has vanished with it.

"Alca, Chapman and myself, as is the Martian habit, walked to the quarry mouth, up a winding and hard stone road. This dreary and desolate region seemed to have a charm. Its expanse of rigid waves of stone, pimpled with sharp excrescences, and as deeply pitted with cavernous grottoes, where no life seemed able to survive, save a stunted herbage, sparsely assembled in vagrant groups, or gathered in thirsty lines around the lip of the still pools, was full of scenic interest, but more deeply eloquent of great geological convulsions.

"Chapman and Alca were in front of me, speaking the Martian tongue, while I stood looking backward every few steps, delighted to trace the broad river of the canal winding through the desolation for miles beyond. Then I noticed how rapid and effortless is motion in Mars. Volition is so easy and penetrating, the body becomes a mere plaything for the mind. Every function, every part is swayed into vitality by the mind. There is the apparent motion of the limbs, but really the whole frame sweeps on as by an intangible process of translation, and the body is transferred to the point the mind desires it to reach almost without fatigue. This gives strength exactly proportioned to Will, and the shorn powers of disease and Time proceed from the creative faculty of thought. The disabling of the body in

Mars by weakness or disease, or accident or age, sprang front a mental discord, an emotional dissonance. Here was the explanation of those disorders that still cling to the Martian life. In this lay also the secret of crime.

"I looked upward to Chapman, who was then peering with hand raised to his eyes at some object before him which the Superintendent had pointed out, and I felt sorrowful that he should be in disagreement with this life. It boded ill. I had begun to love Chapman, and the first sense of suffering I had felt seemed now awakened at the thought of harm coming to him.

"But there was no time for meditation. Chapman and Alca were looking backward and shouting. They beckoned with their arms, and as I gazed I saw between them, and ahead of them a great black object, about which a number of the little workmen were running excitedly like a swarm of ants. I leaped to their position. Chapman exclaimed: 'You remember the meteor we saw. Well, there it is.'

"Extended like a gigantic and deformed missile lay an iron meteorite before us, the same thing as the Siderites that appear in your Museums on Earth. It was yet warm, a crevice spread down into its interior, and it had apparently rolled from the spot of its first impact, since a hammered side, abraded and worn on the hard rock, lay uppermost. It bore the significant pits, thumb-marks and depressions of the terrestrial objects, while streaming striations spread from its front breast where the iron in melting had run like tears over its surface. It measured some four feet in length, and must have weighed many tons.

"Then a curious thing happened, or seemed to happen. Alca, the Superintendent, advanced to it, and bending against it with outstretched arm, muttered a few words, frowned as if in concentrated thought, and— was it credible—the iron object moved. I looked aghast at Chapman, who turned away with what I dismally interpreted was an expression of disgust. I pressed up close to him, and he murmured, 'Was that a miracle? If it was I should like to get back to common sense and jack-screws.'

"We continued upward, and now the terrific gulf piercing the ground for over two terrestrial miles yawned at our feet. The steep precipice, lost in a twilight dusk below, was disconcerting. The blocks of stone were hoisted from the gigantic pit by hoists worked by hand. Here is one of the anomalies of this existence in Mars. Electrical science and its application is understood, great stores of mechanical experience and wisdom can be drawn on, and yet in most of the mechanical work, hand work, the toilsome method of the Pharaohs of Egypt prevails. There are no railroads or trolleys or steam vehicles. The boats are driven by explosive engines, and there are electric carriages of velocity and power. But the latter are infrequent. The canals are numerous, especially about Scandor, and the great trunk canals are broad avenues of traffic.

"The intense swift motion of the Martians meets their needs in most cases. Where hard labor on a mammoth scale is necessary, the little race of *prehistorics* serves all their purposes. The canals are their great engineering feats, and the wonderful telescopes, their triumphs in applied science, their knowledge of the transmutation of the elements,—their greatest intellectual victory,—and Scandor, the City of Glass, their architectural gem and miracle.

"We stood in a line gazing upon the receding roof of the great cavern, the heavy walls left like buttresses to hold up the overlying mountain ridge, and the tiny figures dimly swarming on the distant floor.

"The quarry extends far in under the ridge. Much barren rock is taken out, for the Phosphori rock occurs variously in masses, layers, lenticles, and almond shaped inclusions in the igneous matrix.

"We were to descend, but before we did so the Superintendent led us to the summit of the ridge. From here, with a superb hand telescope, we gazed up a distant land beyond the volcanic area we had surmounted, occupied by farms and villages. It was the North country where the prehistorics dwelt. It seemed peaceful and attractive. Beyond this again we just discerned the shimmering surface of the Great Glacier, the superb train of ice, that comes southward in the winter, and encroaches even upon some of the exposed margins of the land of the prehistorics. Its retreat is rapid in the warm season, and its broad tract is broken by emergent backs of rocks and land, that are seamed with wild flowers. The Martians travel to these oases in the Ocean of Ice, and it is from these flowers that an entrancing perfume is extracted, of which the Martians are extremely fond.

"We lingered on this pinnacle of rock and surveyed a prospect on either side of contrasted and great interest. The land of the Zinipi north of us resembled the fertile hill and valley country of the Genesee River in western New York, the great region south of us a combination of the Snake River country in Idaho, and the fissured ranges of the Silverton Quadrangle in Colorado.

"Between these rose this high partition of castellated rock.

"We descended again to the mouth of the quarry, and, led by the Superintendent, were swung far out from its dizzy sides into the lake of air between them upon a platform, used for an aerial elevator. Chapman clung nervously to me, and complained of a light nausea and dread. I felt only a tonic exhilaration, and as we slowly sank through the shaft of air, crossed by sunlight for some distance, and then passed into the cooler shadows of its deeper parts, where the yet level sun failed to penetrate, I cried aloud with delight, and the abyss around us shouted its salutation back.

"Still we descended, and soon saw back in the deep prolongations of the tunnel the shining walls of this phosphorescent cave. The light glowed so effulgently that it seemed a soft radiant haze, through which came the sound of voices, and in it black figures moved incessantly.

"The method of quarrying is not unlike that of the marble quarries on the earth. Drilling long holes in and under the stone, which from pressure has assumed a rudely cubical cleavage, separates the rock into heavy pieces. These holes are wedged, and the rocks forced off into useful blocks. All is done by hand, and the picture of activity, with workers constantly engaged at their various duties made a singular scene. We walked far into the ever deepening womb of the mountain, while on either hand lateral tunnels, or rather avenues had been pushed, penetrating rich segregations wherever they had been traced, and where also glowed the welcome glow of this lithic lamp.

"The Superintendent explained that the stone was quite unequal in quality, and he told us how the illuminating power of the stone was actually tested in what on the Earth we would call candle powers, but is known on Mars as Ki-kans, or a unit of light derived from a platinum wire one millimetre thick, carrying 100 volts current. We could see the varying radiations, and came upon rayless sections, which from admixture of impurities or imperfect chemical perfection, were deprived of all luminousness.

"Returning, it seemed as if in the sharp convulsions of the crust a flood of light had been somehow absorbed by the rock, and then this light-saturated rock had been overwhelmed and buried out of sight, only to be painfully restored to its first home, in the open skies, by the labor of men.

"But time was pressing. Chapman must reach Scandor, his envoy's errand was important, and bidding the kind Alca good-bye, which the Martians execute by a kiss and an embrace, we came out again into the deep well, and gazed upward past the glistening precipices, irregular with little ledges, and over-reaching cavities, to the distant sky.

"And now a terrible calamity befell us. The Superintendent pointed out a narrow path that led circuitously around the great crags of rock to the top. It was a narrow winding ledge, rising by a mild incline, and circling the pit before it finally reached its brim. In parts it was quite unprotected, but the extraordinary nerves of the men made the achievement of passing out or in the quarry by this means a very simple test of endurance. Even as the

Superintendent alluded to its use, a file of dark figures was just above us, with soldierlike precision marching down to the level we occupied. Chapman banteringly asked me to try it, and I accepted the challenge, urging him to follow.

"We started up. At first the ascent was simple, and the view backward just a little exciting. We continued, and I noticed that the path contracted, and nervously looking on ahead, was startled to find it broken with short gaps, which must be crossed by jumping. I had felt the vague premonitions about Chapman increasing, and somehow, by that intuition which becomes prophetic, in this semi-etherealized constitution of our bodies and minds, in Mars, I knew an impending blow hung over us.

"I looked back and saw Chapman gravely following me. The cheer and laughter had disappeared from his face, the jesting gayety had fled, and he seemed enfeebled. I hastened to him, and he raised his face with a reassuring smile.

"'Dodd,' he said, 'I am dizzy. I feel strangely here,' and he felt his forehead. 'I wonder that it is so. But come! Don't be frightened. It will pass over.' He pushed me from him. For an instant we stood and gazed around us. Far up we saw the outer sunlight beating on the barren exposures of the mountain, around us was black excavated rock, and below the shining walls, faintly blue and pink.

"'Chapman,' I said, 'let us go back. The hoists will take us out.' 'Folly,' was the answer. 'I shall be all right. Why, a Martian has no physical weakness or dread. Come, Dodd, you have not yet acquired the Martian defiance of accident, disease, or death. You are sneaking back under the cover of fear for me.'

"His voice seemed peevish. I looked at him with wonder. He leaped past me, with a forced agility, and sprang on upward. I followed with lightness born of thought, with which the true Martians move.

"On, on, we sped. The narrowing path carried us up until one of those gaps I had noticed came in view. Chapman stopped, and then hearing my approaching steps, ran forward and jumped. His calculation and strength were yet secure and adequate. He safely passed the first break in the pathway, and, as I crossed it with a wide leap, we both still sped on upon an even narrower shelf, which also was more steeply inclined about the jutting prominences of the rocky cliff.

"The next gap was reached, and now the edge of the succeeding length of pathway was not only farther away, but higher up. Chapman, I could see imperfectly, because of a slim projection in my way, had reached the lower side, and, hesitatingly, drew backward. It was his preparation for the leap.

He launched forward. I rushed precipitately upward, feeling the air about me vibrating, it seemed, with an impending disaster. Chapman had landed on the further side of the break, but the cruel, treacherous rock crumbled beneath his impact, and I saw his staggering form turning backward. Another instant and his descending body was below me, plunging to the floor of the abyss. I turned, and then, my son, I felt the marvel of the mind's creative power over matter. I wished myself at the bottom of the quarry where Chapman had fallen, and although the movement of the translation down the pathway seemed apparent, yet I was scarcely parted from him an instant before I was standing and leaning over him in a group of astonished workmen, at the very spot where he lay. He was conscious, but gravely injured. I knelt beside him, and as I raised his head upon my knee, he looked up, and his lips moved; at first he was inarticulate, but soon his words became audible and intelligent.

"'Dodd,' he said, 'this ends me for Mars. Take the papers to the Council at Scandor. They are in the cabin in my desk. They are sealed. I know there is a celestial runaway that is going to strike this planet. I overheard that much at the Patenta. And its direct path, the point of impingement, will be at Scandor. The fires ascending from Scandor are signals that they, too, have divined the disaster. I think so at least! Hurry on! You may see the strangest phenomenon eyes have ever seen. But, Dodd, enough of that. I am turned down for this world. I was not in agreement, as the philosophers call it, and the true mental Martian immunity from accident was not in me. I am injured mortally.'

"He groaned and tried to rise, but his crushed body was incapable. The Superintendent, Alca, had hurried to the spot where the crowding men stood around us ejaculating their amazement. Alca tore open the garment about Chapman, and placing his forehead on the body, poured out as it were, the full tide of his mental sympathy and power.

"I could see the struggle between the mortality of Chapman, born of doubt, and his unfittedness and apathy, and the spiritual power of the brave Superintendent. The flame of life in Chapman would be stimulated or excited, and then flicker and die down. These alterations lasted but a short time. Soon Chapman passed into stupor, and then death supervened, and the strange and seldom known circumstance of death among the supernaturals in Mars was realized.

"Alca kept the body of Chapman, which would be sent back to the City of Light, and cremated in the Temple of Glorification—which I have not seen. He intended to accompany it. He sent me on to Scandor. I had now learned enough of the Martian language to speak, imperfectly. That mental facility, which is the amazing and most wonderful thing in Mars, was perhaps more slowly roused in me. But daily I became known, and more alert and inflamed with thought and the eager intuition of the Martians.

"We started from the great Quarry of Sinsi, and I was alone with the Martians on the porcelain boat, now made by this tragic fate the ambassador from the City of Light to the Council in Scandor.

"The sterile, sinister and yet marvellous region of lava beds, dikes and conic craters suddenly was passed, and the canal moved into the huge forest lands of the Ribi wood.

"This is a beautiful land. Mountain ranges rising from four to six thousand feet cross it, holding broad valleys and plains, or elevated plateaus between them; lakes and rivers pass through it, and villages and towns with a mixed population of the supernaturals and the prehistorics are frequent. The canals cross the great region in many directions. The trunk line I followed was carried up and down by systems of locks of astounding magnitude and perfection. Great lakes were made convenient feeders, and rivers were also tapped to keep the water levels constant in the canals. The weather was that of a semi-tropical paradise, and the late flowers of the Ribi filled the air with fragrance.

"Quickly we approached Scandor. It was a clear, calm day when we emerged from the Ribi country, and the pilot pointed out to me the distant hills, almost purple in a twilight haze, which encircled the Valley of the City of Scandor. The country we had entered was a fertile farm country, where great plantations of the Rint, and vineyards of the Oma grapes were established, and where great flocks of the Imilta dove, almost the only meat eaten by the Martians, are raised. The enormous flocks of this snow-white bird were strangely beautiful. They made clouds in the air, and their purring notes when they settled in white blankets over the fields, were heard pulsating over long distances.

"Finally we came to the last tier of locks at the summit of which my curiosity was to be satisfied by a view of the great City of Scandor, the City of Glass.

"It was night when our china boat floated upon the waters of the last lock that completed the ascent, and immediately below the observatory Station or Settlement of Scandor. I was standing on the deck of the boat, watching impatiently the slowly rising tide upon which we were borne upward. I could at first see as we ascended the towers of the observatory station. Above me, looking at us with interest, on the walls of the lock, was a company of Martians. The night was cloudy, and the lights of the hastening satellites were but intermittently evident. Gradually my head passed upward beyond the obstructing interference of wall and gate and fence, and the glorious and unimaginable splendor of the City of Scandor, like some monstrous continental opal, lay before me in the immediate valley.

"The glistening panes of water below me marked the places of the descending line of locks. Around me were the buildings of the Scandor Observatory, and to the right and left swept the forested slopes of a circular range which, as I later saw, ranged about in one amphitheatrical circuit the, great vale of Scandor. But only an instant's glance could be spared for this detail. The divine City glowing below me seemed to magnetize attention, and control, through its wonderfulness each wavering attitude of interest. My son, the eye of man never beheld so astonishing a picture. Imagine a city reaching twenty miles in all directions built of glass variously designed, interrupted by tall towers, pyramids, minarets, steeples, light, fantastic and beautiful structures, all aflame, or rather softly radiating a variously colored glory of light.

"Imagine this great area of building, penetrated by broad avenues, radiating like the spokes of a wheel from a center where rose upward to the sky a colossal amphitheatre. Imagine these roads, delineated to the eye by tall chimneys or tubes of glass through which played an electric current, converting each one into a lambent pillar. Imagine between these paths of greenish opalescence the squares of buildings of domed, arched and castellated roofs, pierced and starred, and spread in lines and patterns of white electric lamps. The noble proportions of the larger buildings, the graceful outlines of turreted or campanulate erections, and the smaller houses were all defined. I could see canals or rivers of water winding through the City spanned by arches of flame, and even the symmetrical disposition of the dark-leaved trees was visible.

"But the night was still further turned to day, for above the City, high in the velvet black empyrean were suspended thousands of glass balloons, each emitting the Geissler-like illumination that marked the lines of streets. So full and opulent was the flood of light, that the summit I had reached, the encircling hills, and the farther side of the saucer-shaped valley where Scandor lay, were bathed in an equally diffused radiation.

"But, as if the heavenly marvel might still further startle and amaze and charm me, from the City rose the swelling chords of choruses; billows of sound, softened by distance, beat in melodious surges on the high encompassing lands.

"I stood mute and transfixed. It seemed a beatific vision. If the very air had been filled with ascending choruses of angels, if the dark zenith had opened and revealed the throne of the Almighty, it would have seemed but a congruous and expected climax.

"Long I gazed, and slowly, very slowly became conscious of the great numbers of people about me, and that they were being augmented by new arrivals. The porcelain barge I had come in from the City of Light, was moored now to the side of the lock. I had disembarked, carrying almost mechanically in my hand, the chest in which the communications from the Patenta to the Council were locked.

"It was perhaps only a short interval before the pilot woke me from my trance, saying in Martian: 'This is the Observation Hill of Scandor. These are Scandor's Observatories. I hear there is seen by the observers some approaching danger in the heavens. These citizens of Scandor are crowding from the City to hear the latest reports. There is a messenger from the Council here waiting on the observers. I will bring him to you, and you and the messenger can at once be conveyed to the Council.'

"I looked at him speechless, yet unable to again realize I lived and breathed in another world. It seemed as if a sudden motion, a cry, a whisper even, would break the chrysalis of sleep about me, and plunge me into void and nothingness.

"The pilot left me, and I saw him thread his way amongst the lines of people, moving toward the dark walls of the observatory that covered the hill. At long intervals rockets rose from the opposite rim of the great circular ridge around the City, scarring the deep, inky vault about us with lines of fire. They ascended to an enormous distance. Almost instantly these were apparently answered by similar rockets in other colors from the hill I stood on.

"There was a sudden movement about me. The pilot had returned. With him came the messenger. I flung my absorption from me. I was a Martian. The light of recognition came back again to my eyes—my tongue was loosened, my senses accommodated themselves to the stupendous circumstances about me. I spoke first.

"'Mindo,' (the name of the pilot), 'I am ready to accompany my guide to the City. Will you go with us?'

"'No! Heboribimo,' (your excellency), 'I must stay at the locks. I shall descend to the City in the boat to-morrow. This man will bring you to the canal. I advise haste. There is great excitement and dread in Scandor. Mars is in the path of a comet.'

"I turned to my guide, a beautiful youth, not dressed as the citizens of the City of Light, but clothed in a tight fitting doublet of a creamy blue, with short trunks of yellow, and on his feet were sandals. He saluted me, and together we descended the broad boulevard between the widely separated lustres that became more crowded as they massed like a progressive deepening of color into the eddying splendors of the City itself.

"Again I realized how swift is motion in Mars. We wished to reach the City, and we glided to it by the rapid propulsion of desire. The broad way was filled with lines and groups of peoples clustering to the hilltop—and over the far-reaching slopes I could see the awaiting throngs. My guide pointed to the constellation of Perseus, and I could discern a nebulous mass of considerable diameter from which proceeded a wisp-like exhalation, just a phantasmal fan of phosphorescence, behind it.

"The glory of the City fell around us now; we were in its broad streets beneath the towering pillars of light that framed them in a fence of splendor. On we pressed, but I glanced from side to side, noting the great glass houses and buildings, here colonnades of translucent opalescent beauty, made up of hollow tubes of glass holding an interior illumination, and clambered over by vines whose expanding leaves formed a tracery of silhouettes upon their sides.

"Still on, past porticos and under arches, through open forum-like squares, from which were elevated the great glass globes I have described, which hung lamp-like in the sky,—past palaces and arcades, blocks of low stores in iridescent tints, and long, straight fronts of white opaque buildings, through occasional tunnels into which we plunged as into a sea of radiance, and on, out, past a few squares of black umbrageous trees that seemed like dead coals laid on the heat quivering hearth of a furnace, past minarets of curling, entwined filagrees of glass threads, past dull or darker areas where the huge glass factories were built, their forges glowing like Cyclops' eyes in the night, and from which was produced the colossal sum of manufacture, which this great City embodied.

"It was a strange bewilderment of marvels, and from it all, as if it were its interior motive and cause, sprang light. It was electric in origin, conveyed in some peculiar manner from a great source of power, in the high falls of Zenapa, near the City. But this I learned later.

"I divined that we were approaching the center of the city. Soon, indeed, I saw before me the sparkling walls of the amphitheatre I had descried from the hill of Observation at the locks. Here it is, that the great plays, the gigantic concerts, the operas, and services of the Pan-Tan are held. It was a seraphic, astounding picture. It rose in the midst of a great square of many acres in extent, where the light, purposely subdued, allowed its dazzling beauty subdued isolation. How wonderful! I stopped. For one instant, before hurrying on, I gazed upon a miracle of constructive and decorative art. One hundred columns of red glass rose upward, and between them was a wall, in tiers of green glass arches, and on the keystone of each a pink globe of fire. From the pillars sprang, in an inverted terrace formation, metallic brackets, carrying gorgeous chandeliers of a red bronze; the largest chandeliers were at the very upper edge of the building, and the cascade of light thus shed upon the splendid fabric was indescribably magnificent.

"But there was small time for wonder or examination. We swept on through the shadowy gardens about it, and my guide quickly brought me to the Hall of the Council, a low, inconspicuous building of yellow brick, one of the few discordant architectural notes in the whole city.

"The doors of the single chamber, which embraced all the interior space, swung open, and I stood on the threshold of a shallow, rectangular depression, surrounded on all sides with benches, and holding in its central area a long table, at which, beneath tall lamps, sat, perhaps, a dozen men and one woman. Opposite to my point of view, in a niche upon the further wall, was the colossal figure of the Deity I had seen in the Patenta at the City of Light.

"The faces of the twelve men turned to us as we entered. The herald announced my errand with the customary salutation of 'Hebori bimo.' I was invited to descend to the central table. I advanced, and laying Chapman's chest, with its sealed communications upon the table, spoke:

"'I am a stranger. I have come to your world from the Earth. I bring news, celestial news, from the astronomers of the City of Light. I had a companion to whom all this was entrusted.' He was killed in the quarries of Tiniti. I came on, bidden so to do by Alca, the Superintendent. The papers of the Wise Men of the Patenta are here.'

"I laid the chest upon the table. My speech was yet unformed, and perhaps upon the delicate and intellectual faces before me, there dwelt, with the transient influence of a passing thought, a smile of sympathy or amusement. Then a young being at the head of the table exclaimed in Martian:

"'Welcome, stranger. All who come to us are soon made one with ourselves. The Martian spirit is that of salutation and friendship. We have heard of the discoveries in the new commotions in planetary space. Our own astronomers have announced them. This great City of Scandor, the product of many centuries' toil and invention, is apparently doomed. It lies in the path, certainly defined and determined by observers, of a small cometary mass, which will plunge upon it a rain of rock and iron. Even now this approaching body grows more and more visible in the sky. The astronomers are working at the problem, hoping some deflection, some interpositional mercy will carry off this disturbing incidence. But if we are to be destroyed, if there is no escape from the singular fortune of annihilation by an inrushing stream of meteoric bodies, then warning, through proclamation, shall be made, and our citizens will move out of the city to Asco, and the islands of Pinit.'

"He ceased; upon him the expectant faces of the others, assembled about the table, were fixed, and a visible tremor of dismay and grief seemed to convulse them. A few covered their faces with their hands, others stood up and gazed at the benignant colossus in bronze at the end of the room, while others, motionless, still maintained their attitude of attention.

"The presiding officer, with a slight inclination of the body, raised his hand, and addressing me, said: 'You shall be the guest of our City, and if it must be that this great capital of Mars must succumb to this mysterious invasion, if this place, so long a marvel of beauty, shall be succeeded by a heap of burning stones, then you shall be our companion in pilgrimage. Remain with us until the end of this strange circumstance is known.'

"As he finished, a noise of indescribable lamentation from a multitude of voices broke upon our ears—the sound of running feet and sharp cries of amazement, crashed in upon the half ominous silence about us.

"I turned instinctively to my guide. He stood statue-like beside me, with a stealing pallor crossing his face, and then, the doors of the apartment swung open, and loud voices were heard crying, 'The Peril comes. Stand forward. To the Hills!'

"Panic, that nameless associated mental terror of the unknown and the impending, which on Earth spreads fever-like through multitudes, had arisen amongst the Martians, and hurrying crowds were hastening in a wild retreat from the City to the hills.

"All thought of the Council, of my errand, or of the new relation I had been graciously accorded, disappeared from my mind. Frightened by the sudden premonition of destruction, bewildered by the torrent of new sensations, and even yet only half confident that my existence in the new world was altogether real, I was impelled to spring forward. Reaching the doors, hands shot out around me, and I was swept in the tide of running forms.

"It was a living stream of manifold complexity. Only for one moment did I lose consciousness. The next I was struggling to escape from the spreading tentacles of this involved current. I leaped to the projection of a low pedestal, upon which an unfinished construction or group of statues was in progress. Holding my exposed position for an instant, I wrenched myself clear of the pulsating throngs, and succeeded in gaining the low summit above me. Here I was free to look around me. My guide was gone, the Council House was lost to view; I was alone. Below passed the surging crowd, made up of youths and girls, with few older men or women, many beautiful, all expressing the Martian distinction, but now strangely bewildered and uncontrolled. It was a reversed emotional picture from that buoyant, frenzied throng that a few weeks ago carried me into the Hall of the Patenta.

"Faces were turned toward the sky, and hands, as if in ejaculation, were waved up and down, or thrust in significant indices toward that fatal blurred blot of splendor in the heavens. I followed their direction. The approaching nebula had grown sensibly since an hour ago. It glittered, the size of a shield, and a light coruscation seemed emanating from its edges. The faces of the multitude were justified. The mass above us was a train of celestial missiles, hurling toward Mars. Its contact seemed more and more imminent. I felt a nameless terror. The thought of isolation in this new world, the unknown awfulness of this planetary disturbance, the sudden extinction of the hopes that were feeding my heart with a new life, and the forecasting of the impossible agonies of universal death in this great, strange place I had so wonderfully entered, overcame me. I fell sobbing to the glassy floor on which I was standing. It was again a new proof of my assumption of the ecstatic nature of these children of light and music, impulse and inspiration.

"The convulsion passed. I felt stronger, and was quickened with a keenly prudent determination to escape from the city, find my way back to the Hill of Observation, and if possible, send you, my son, my last experience before all had become silence.

"I could see the regular ascent of the rockets from the distant hill. I found the streets about me almost emptied, the white, lustrous river of life had passed. I descended to the pavement. The way past the splendid Amphitheatre was easily found, and then I hastened, guided by a dumb instinct of direction, toward the still ascending rockets. I came to the broad Boulevard which led to the Hill of Observation, and went on, now plainly controlled by the sweeping avenue of lamps about, and in front of me.

"I shall not pause to recount the success of my application to the astronomers to use the transmitters of the wireless telegraphy, which are as fully perfected here as at the City of Scandor.

"As my message ends, the dawn ascends from the wide margins of the Ribi country. I am stunned with drowsiness. The Sun's rays have extinguished the scintillant peril in the skies. But the order has gone forth to leave the City, to camp upon the hills, the City of Scandor is doomed, and the area of destruction it embraces is the diametral measure of the——"

I heard no more. Overcome with fatigue, exposure and increasing pulmonary weakness, of which I had had painful premonitions, I fainted at the table, and fell to the floor of the damp and inclement room.

My assistants aver that the transmission ceased almost the next moment upon my collapse, and the unfinished sentence of my father's message can be readily understood as implying that the foreign body, or Swarm, which was destined to strike Mars, had been determined as having about the amplitude of the City of Scandor.

Days lengthened into weeks, weeks to months, but though unflinchingly watched by night and day, no further message was received. I had become weaker, pale and lifeless. The terrible malady made its inroads upon a frame unable to meet its savage or insidious attacks. This weakness was aggravated by the excitement produced by the singular experience I had passed through. My nerves had undergone a strain quite unusual, and the interior sense of elation, reacting its fits of extreme mental despondency dislocated my system, and accelerated the gliding virus of disease inundating the capillaries of circulation and breaking down the tissues with fever and consumption.

CHAPTER VI

Miss Dodan came more and more frequently to see me. The thought of my physical depression, the revulsion of hopelessness over my changing lineaments made the love I bore her more painful and enervating. I tried hard to conceal my fears over my condition. But Miss Dodan had been observant. Her developing affections became daily more tender and delicate, and her solicitude evinced itself in many charming, thoughtful ways that added only a more poignant sadness to my sufferings.

I was, indeed, tortured by the conflicting aims life seemed to furnish me. On the one hand was the necessity of continuing, if I could, my communications with my father; on the other, the duty I owed myself to abandon all for the woman I truly loved, and to renovate and establish my health so that I might woo and win, and marry her.

It was, in a sense, an ethical question, but it was quite as hard to determine by ordinary arguments whether I could have any permission to violate my promise to my father, as it was to estimate the exact measure of my obligations to myself and Miss Dodan. An incident occurred that dissipated this dilemma, sent Miss Dodan to England, and left me at Christ Church to receive the last message from my father before the sickness had fully developed that now has laid its searching and remorseless veto upon any further life or happiness for me in this world.

Miss Dodan and myself were seated together upon a bench drawn up in the sunshine at the foot of the Observatory, watching with delight the distinct changing sea, the plumes of smoke from diminished steamers, and the white glory of full-rigged ships. It was the autumn of the southern country, and the dreamy spell of the declining days fell softly upon the material tissues of nature, as well as on the acquiescent spirit of man.

"Father," said Miss Dodan, uncertainly, while she formed her hand into an improvised tube, and looked through it on the peaceful scene at our feet, "has been telling me of my birthplace in Devonshire. It must be very beautiful, more beautiful than it is here. But there is no sea, and it seems to me now that I should die without it; it is the very soul and voice, too, of all this picture!" She spread out her arms, and half willfully threw back the one nearest me, until it swept over my head, and I caught and kissed the opened palm.

"Yes," I replied, "the sea relieves everything about or near it, from the humiliation of commonness. The stamp of distinction rests on its printless waves. It was the first surface of the earth, and its primal regency has never been lost or forfeited;" a suspicion crossed my mind: "How was it your father spoke of Devonshire. I never knew before that you came from that pearl of the countries of England. Would you like to see it?"

My voice half sank, and the hitherto unsuspected fact that Mr. Dodan had observed my physical danger, and now was planning to interrupt his daughter's intimacy and hallucination for a poor, failing man, struggling with an impossible problem, and a mortal malady, seemed suddenly understood by me. I turned to her a face of questioning concern. Her eyes were still fixed upon the distant, pulsating sea. "No," she answered, half nonchalantly. "I suppose not, and yet—why not! I have only known this country; to cross the great ocean, to see the capital of the world, to learn the great wonders of its palaces and temples, to see its multitudes, to see the Queen. Ah! to see the Queen!"

Her hands folded tightly together across her brow, she looked the very embodiment of reverent expectation, and the blushing roses on her cheeks, the lovelight in her eyes seemed to deepen for an instant, and then pale slightly, as she turned to me only to see me bury my head in my hands, holding back the cry of stifled hope that often before had leaped to my lips, but never had before so nearly passed them.

"Oh, Bradford," she cried, "would you mind so much! I would soon be back again. And then, you know, this awful telegraphic work would be over, and we could be happy together without a thought of that cold, far-away Mars!"

We talked on together till the dusky night had begun to gather its shadows about us, and Mars, that marvellous spot of light from whose untouched continents the waves of magnetic oscillation might even then be starting on their pathless transit across the abyss of space, destined for my ear, began to shine above us.

It was clear to me now that Mr. Dodan had been carefully nursing in his daughter a desire to see England and the Queen, and her own little birthplace, and that he had formed a resolution to separate us, for his daughter's best interests, as he thought.

I suffered from a very proud, sensitive nature, perhaps unwholesomely intensified by the lonely life I had led, and a peculiar sense of my difference from other people.

This revelation, so unwelcome, so fraught with painful anticipations, roused my pride to a sharp climax of revolt, disdain and defiance. Miss Dodan should go,—I should urge it. I would applaud and hasten it, there would be no weakness, no supplication, no obstacles on my part. Let death write his inerrant claim to me, let it be recognized; Mr. Dodan need not be disturbed as to my absolute self-control.

The very acerbity of my coming misery, through Miss Dodan's absence, fully realized by me, seemed now only to add a desperation of assumed indifference and gayety to all my actions. I argued against delay, and dwelt with excellent effect upon the charms of the visit. I assumed that Miss Dodan needed the change, that the educational value of such an experience would be incalculable.

Mr. Dodan was frankly surprised and pleased. This unexpected support and enthusiastic commendation of his plan was something he gratefully accepted, and he assumed a new manner toward me. He ascribed to me a power of self-renunciation which won his ardent approval and admiration.

The day was at last fixed. Miss Dodan, young, appreciative, and curious, was elated at the prospect of the voyage, and, momentarily, at least, forgot her first reluctance to desert me. The preparations were all completed. I need not dwell upon all the detail of that last week. It was a cruel ordeal for me, but no one would have suspected my real anguish. I seemed the most thoughtful of all, the most naturally buoyant and hopeful for the success of the trip. I forgot nothing. The telegraph station was not, however, neglected. I watched at night, and during the hours of my absence my assistant was persistently present in the tower.

At last the steamer sailed away from the wharf at Port Littelton. The last moments I passed alone with Miss Dodan were sacred, sweet memories; all that I have now.

Mr. and Mrs. Dodan and Miss Dodan were waving their handkerchiefs from the deck as I turned sorrowfully back to Christ Church. I realized that I had seen Miss Dodan for the last time, and that when she returned to New Zealand, she would only find me gone. There was but one duty now. To resume, if possible, the communications with my father, and prepare the story of my experience and discoveries, and leave it to the world.

I went back to the Observatory. I was again alone. A reaction of despondency overwhelmed me, and it was coincident with a hemorrhage, which left me weak and nervous. I resumed my watching at the station. I seemed to anticipate a new message. I endured peculiar and excruciating excitement, a tense suspense of desire and prevision that deprived me of appetite and sleep, and accelerated the ravages of the disease, that now, victorious over my weakened, nervous force, began the last stages of its devastating advance.

It was a clear, cold night of exquisite severity and beauty—May 20, 1894, that the third message came from my father. It was announced, as had been all the others, by the sudden response of the Morse receiver. A few nights before, grasping at a vague hope that I might again reach him with the magnetic waves at my command, I had launched into space the single sentence: "Await me! Death is very near." The message that now startled my ears began with an exact answer to that trans-abysmal despatch:

"My son, the thought of your death fills me with happiness. Surely you will come to this wonderful and unspeakable world, you will see me again, and I you, but under such new circumstances! My heart yearns for you immeasurably. Come! Come quickly! To press you to my heart, to speak with you, to teach you the new things, and Oh! more than all, to bring you to your mother. For, Tony, she is found; my search is ended. I have discovered her whom the cruel mystery of Death on earth so sharply removed from us, in youth and radiance. I have not yet revealed myself. The joy of anticipation surpasses thought or words. I have hastened back from seeing her, whom to leave in this paradise imparts the one pang I have known in this new life, hastened again to the Hill of Observation that now looks on the cruel ruin, the emptiness of desolation, where once was the City of Scandor. Let me tell you all:

"When I sent you my last message I was at the Tower of Observation. As the last wave was emitted from the transmitter, the hand of Superintendent Alca, whom I met at the mines, was laid upon my shoulder. I looked up in surprise. He answered my questioning glance: 'I did not return with Chapman. There was no need of it. A barge going to the City of Light took the body. I explained everything in a letter to the Council. I was distressed over the news I had received of the approach of the cometary mass, which I have detected myself, and I hurried after you in my own kil-chow (the name of the little porcelain steamers), anxious to see this terrible thing. Let us go out and watch the wonder. Whatever happens we shall remain together. I am from Scandor myself, and though I might have been safer at the mines, I could not stay there in the crisis.'

"We descended to the ground and walked out over the hillside. The encircling range of high country about Scandor is, perhaps, one thousand feet high. Its crest is a low swell, that beyond the city falls away in broken, irregular slopes to the country of the Ribi on one side, and to far outstretched plains on almost every other side. This dome was covered with the people of Scandor, fleeing from the doomed city. The long lines of moving figures were issuing from the city through its numerous boulevards, and crowding the spaces on the hilltops. The astronomers knew exactly now the nature of the approaching mass, its orbit, spacial extent and weight. Their proclamation had been prepared and pasted all over the city, announcing its certain destruction, but that the area of devastation would only embrace the city, that the cometary visitor was a narrow train or procession of meteors of stone and iron, that the force of impact would be considerable, enough to crush to the ground the glassy splendor of the beautiful city, and that beyond its limits there would be almost no falls.

"Beautiful, indeed, was Scandor in the morning light. It lay before us shining with a hundred hues. How can I tell you of its exquisite perfection! Its arrangement expressed a color scheme simple and effective. The amphitheatre rose in the center, an opalescent yellow; the boulevards spaced with trees, stretched out in radiating lines from it, defined by the blue lines of ornamental metal pillars which held the lamps; from point to point, piercing the air from the shady peaks or squares shot up also the needles of metal holding the curious electric globes, while at regular intervals blue domes like gigantic azure bubbles interrupted the streets of square and colonnaded houses, that began around the amphitheatre, with pale saffron tones, and grew in intensity until the edges of the huge populous ellipse were laid like a deep orange rim upon the green country side. The light falling upon this reflected, refracted and dispersed, seemed to convert it into a liquid and faintly throbbing lake of color, cut up into segments by the dark lanes or streets of trees.

"And this was to be crushed and crumbled to the ground. The houses and all the constructions are built of glass bricks laid in courses, as with you on the earth, a soluble glass forming the cement that holds them in contact and together. The huge glass factories making this formed a black circle in one part of the City.

"It was now day, and the meteoric nebula was invisible. All day the people came crowding to the hills. At last, as we gazed in bewildered admiration at the strange multitudes about us, the sound of distant music, the organ-like swell of a titanic chorus approaching was heard. Far away down the boulevard, on whose apex we stood, we saw a marching retinue of men and women surrounding a platform borne on the shoulders of men. The platform held the upright figures of the Council amongst whom, distinguished by a blue chalcal tunic bound about him by yellow cords, was the noble being I had seen in the Council chamber on the night of my arrival in Scandor.

"How marvellous it all seemed. The sense of unreality, of dreamland again overpowered me, a wild horror like some mad possession seized me. I shook convulsively, and covered my face in my hands, stricken through and through with a nameless repining misery of doubt, of apprehension, of dismay. It was the last struggle of readjustment between my memories of earth, my identity as a man on the earth, and this new life I had entered. Alca caught me affectionately and placed the acrid bean I had tasted in the City of Light in my mouth. The black suffocation passed, and as I slowly returned to realization and serenity I opened my eyes upon the city, now dead and silent, but blazing with all its lights, awaiting desolation, dressed in its sumptuous glory like some princely captive on whom the doom of immolation, before an unappeasable deity, had suddenly fallen. It was night fall.

"Suddenly a flash, a short piercing note, a loud report, and the sky above us seemed crowded with glowing missiles. The impact from the first arrivals of the cometary body upon the outer envelopes of the Martian atmosphere had begun. A loud shout of attention, surprise and half extemporized terror rose from the multitudes about us. It was a breathless moment. The oncoming shoals shot forward in rapid jets of fire now clouded together in igneous masses, now separated in disjointed streaks and radiant clusters of snapping, shining bolts.

"As yet the material rushing in upon us failed, in most instances, to reach the ground in solid forms. It was burned up in the air. The spectacle was surpassingly strange. The air before us was weaved with crossing shafts, threads, and traces of phosphorescent light. Behind this veil still shone with responsive beauty the great city, while rising occasionally in bursts of color, we could see the alarm rockets from the opposite hills penetrate the entering flood of light with frivolous and extinguished protests.

"About half an hour after the glory reached us, and as on all sides the country shone in spectral illumination, a great mass, decrepitating with minute explosions along its oncoming side, plunged down upon the noble amphitheatre of glass. A dreadful sound of crashing stone followed, and then, rapidly fired from the aerial batteries, came still more of the dark, half ignited bodies, bathed in hurrying streams of evanescent blades, and splinters of light.

"And now the destructive bombardment had really begun. The celestial downpour increased, the valley below us sent upward the detonations of exploding meteorites and the harsh reverberating crash and overthrow of glass fabrics. The lights of the city were brokenly extinguished and the pitiless hail of ruin continued with increasing fierceness.

"It was an awful, glorious scene. The vault of the sky emptying itself in an avalanche of flame, while from within the wide stream of projectiles, collisions caused by some accident of deflection originated interior spots of sudden blazing light. The irregular and separated shocks of sound from the falling city now ran together in a continuous roar of dislocated and broken walls, towers, parapets and citadels. Coruscations sprang out from the yet heated masses, accumulating on the ground, as they became incessantly struck by new accessions. The ground trembled with ceaseless fulminations and impingement, the atmosphere seemed saturated with sulphurous odors, and the panoramic flow of fluctuating splendor shed a day-like brightness upon the upturned faces of the startled and stupefied multitude.

"All night long the invasion continued. The area of destruction, exactly as the astronomers had defined it, was confined to the long elliptical basin in which Scandor lay. Beyond it hardly a branch upon the trees was broken, though occasional erratic bombs shot over us and fell miles away along the borders of the canals.

"As the morning dawned, the shower discontinued, a few laggards fell in scattering confusion over the prostrate city, and the sun climbing the eastern sky sent its peaceful reassuring light upon a cairn-like heap of desolation. The chilled surface of the fallen meteorites were broken up by areas of glowing cinder-like surfaces. The glittering and opaline city of glass, the City of Scandor, capital of the Martian world, was buried beneath the scorching and stony fragments of a minor comet, or some diminished and wandering meteor train which suddenly issuing from the unknown depths of space had descended with mathematical precision upon the treasure city of the planet.

"The Martian legions remained on the hilltops, sombered and silent. The awful reality, impregnable and drear, before them had changed their spirit, and they looked into each other's faces with bewilderment.

"I had stayed with Alca throughout the night, and I now turning to him said:

"'Let us go! What can we do here? Let us walk away for awhile. I am dizzy with terror.'

"'Yes,' he answered, and tears seemed filling his eyes, 'we will go. We will walk out into the hill and river country beyond the canal. Many are wandering over the country now. The farmers will harbor us and the beauty of the lanes will bring us cheerfulness.'

"And so we went away, hastening with the Martian velocity of motion until as the sun hung in the zenith, we had reached a hillside sloping upon a meadow space through which passed the clear but sluggish waters of a wide stream. A tulip-like grass was distributed in the heavy luxuriant growth of the meadow, which bore upon pendant threads a blue bell-like flower. A gentle wind, rising and falling, swept over them, lifting and blowing out the cups as it passed off to the surface of the water and printed it with plashes of ripples. A piece of wood pushed out from the hillside, the trees that formed it struggling out into the meadow in a broken succession of individuals like a line of men. Here, leaning against the last tree trunk that stood quite alone in advance of its companions, was a young woman, her arms folded above the cap—like the Grecian cassos—that imperfectly held her hair, and dressed in a yellow tunic and the half seen leggings of meshed chalcal thread—a lovely picture of meditation.

"I caught Alca's arm in a sudden wave of desire and excitement. It was the impulse of love, the first burning of its sacred fire I had known in Mars, and it was the intense certainty of recognition that made it so impetuous. My Son, your Mother was before me!

"The same glorious beauty I had known on earth covered her, and like a mystic light shone from her face and person. I was myself again, young, and she was the same. The impelling sense of a superhuman Destiny bringing us together again in this new world, forced from me an ejaculation of thankfulness. The cry was not loud, but audible to her ears, and she turned toward us. Yes! it was Martha, as I knew her in those raptured days of love on the banks of the Hudson before disease and weakness and age had stolen the bloom from her cheeks, the light from her eyes, and the fair presentiment of charm and perfection from her body. She did not see me perhaps clearly. Certainly she did not recognize me. An instant's scrutiny and her face turned again to the open exposure of hill and field, stream and cloud-flecked sky.

"Alca had observed my gestures of delight, and, perhaps reading my thoughts by that intuition of mind so wonderful in the Martians, pushed me toward her gently and moved away from us toward the brink of the river.

"I stood for a moment hesitating, overwhelmed with the marvel of this new thing. I stole on, and finally pushing aside the high grown grass, was at her side—at the side of the very form and feature of the woman who had taught me on earth the worth of living and the meaning and the glory of rectitude.

"She was breathing fast, her bosom rising and falling with quick respirations, and her cheeks flushed with color, made a delicious foil to the pearly tone of her face, concealed on her neck and forehead by the escaping tresses of her dark hair.

"I drew back, trembling with anticipation, my heart beating, and my clasped hands folded on my breast in an agony of restraint. She was talking, talking to herself in the low musical voice of the Martians. The wind had ceased, a dark shadow from a crossing cloud moved toward us from the river over the blue sprinkled field, a haze stole upward from the farther view, and, bending at the margin of the water the figure of Alca bathed in light, seemed to watch us like some calm incarnate response to my own hopes and prayers.

"'How beautiful, how wonderful it is!' her arms dropped from her head, the body bent forward to the earth, she knelt; 'but must it always be as it is!

Shall not the companion of my days come to this dear place? The light of sun and moon and stars seems as it always seemed on Earth, but there does not come to me the divine touch of affection, that intimate feeling of oneness and self-surrender that was mine with Randolph on the Earth. A strength unknown to me before, a power of enjoyment, a motion that is ecstacy, thought, feeling, language, all strong, radiant, supreme, but yet loneliness! Memory of the things of Earth hardly remains, except where love prints its firm expression. Randolph, my husband, and Bradford, my boy, to me are deathless. Why can it not be that they should be here also? Can the purposes of divine love be fulfilled by this separation? Shall all the powers of this new life, this beautiful and sinless Nature be wasted for the want of love which holds both Nature and the soul in place, in harmony, in adoration of the One enduring Thought?

"'How the long years have rolled by since I have left the Earth, and how, amid all the pleasurable things of this serene and hopeful life, the hidden loneliness has denied it the last completing touch of joy! Only as I still dare to believe, that the flight of years must end his aging days on Earth, and that the eternal destiny of married souls is an eternal union, and that his reincarnation here shall bring us into a new and better, richer, deeper harmony of mind and tastes and thoughts; only as the belief grows stronger with passing time, can I, so surrounded with peace and happiness, in this countryside of quiet work and gentle cares, bear longer this awful isolation, the nights of prayerful hope, the days of still enduring hope.

"'How beautiful it is to live, to watch the changing seasons in this strange new world untouched by sickness or death or sin. And yet,' she convulsively clasped her face, 'what beauty, what peace, what sinlessness can replace the only life—the Life of Love?

"'And then my boy! Can it be possible that I may see him! Why, now he will seem only a brother in this new youth in which I have been born, and yet—and yet—the mother feeling is unchanged; the old yearning, just as when I left him a boy upon the Earth seems as great as ever.

"'Oh! when shall this waiting all end in our reunion—father, mother, son—and all strong and glad in youth and hope?'

"She rose and stretched out her arms toward some phantasy of thought or fancy in the air above her, and then a song of recall from a distance floated along the meadow and the river's banks, a sweet, joyous, beckoning melody, that compelled the ear to listen, and the feet to follow.

"Martha half turned—I was dazed with wonder—I did not wish to speak. I could not then have revealed myself. It was all too marvellous, too hard to comprehend. The old doubts of my reality, of the realness of everything I had seen, surged up again, and swept over me in a tide of disillusion.

"Was I dreaming; in the death from Earth had I passed into a wild phantasmagoria of mental pictures, some endless dream where the lulled soul encountered again, as visions, all it may have hoped for, all its unconscious cerebration had limned on the interior canvases of the mind, to be reviewed, as in a sleep, where every detail met the test of curiosity—except that last test—waking? Should I awake?

"I sprang forward and beat myself, in a sort of fury of doubt against the trees about me. The resistance was secure and certain. Pain—it seemed a kind of bliss, as the guarantee of my flesh and blood existence—came to me and in my paroxysms the torn skin of my body bled. I looked at the red stains with exultation. I felt the aches of physical concussion, with a real rapture.

"This life was real, was dual—body and mind—as on Earth, and the woman hastening before me along the marge of the rippling stream—I listened in a kind of feverish anticipation of its silence, for the low cadence of water passing over pebbles—was Martha! It must be true! What agency of superhuman cruelty could thus deceive me? No! my eyes were faithful, and the air, thrilling with the distant song, brought nearer to my ears the answering call of my wife!

"She was far distant. I ran from tree to tree in the wooded back ground and traced her to a little hamlet where a group of Martians awaited her. They turned up a narrow lane singing, and I lost them.

"I returned to Alca, pensively standing on the hill we had first descended, and said nothing of the strange revelation. I contrived to learn from him the name of the little village, and the nature of its inhabitants. He called it Nitansi, and said it had been one of the old spots where migrating souls from other worlds once entered Mars.

"'A few,' he added, 'come there now, though rarely, and the people cultivate flowers in great farms, and formerly sent them to Scandor. I think I saw them moving now along the fields at the riverside. We must go back. I shall go down the canal to Sinsi. I know the Council of Scandor will resolve to rebuild the city.'"

The message closed. I rose and staggered backward into the arms of Jobson. A severe hemorrhage ensued, and slowly thereafter the darkening doors of life began to close upon me. Disease had won its way against all the force of life.

It has been my task during these last weeks of life to write this account of these wonderful experiences, and to leave them to the world as an assurance—to how many will it give a new delight in living, to how many will it remove the bitterness of living, to how many may it bring resignation and hope—that the blight of Death is only an incident in a continuous renewal of Life.

(End of Mr. Dodd's MS.)

Note by Mr. August Bixby Dodan.

Mr. Dodd died January 20, 1895. He never recovered from the severe shock caused by hemorrhage, after receiving the second message from his father and recorded above. He appreciated the imminence of death acutely, and struggled to complete, as he has, the narrative of his life. My daughter was not again seen by Mr. Dodd, though he received several letters from her, which were found beneath his pillow after his demise.

I was with Mr. Dodd constantly during the latter days of his illness, and then promised him that I should secure the publication of his remarkable story.

I am not willing to hazard any conjecture as to the more extraordinary features of this narrative. I can very positively, however, affirm my complete confidence in Mr. Dodd's honesty. I knew both his father and himself very well, and through a long intimacy found them both consistently conforming to a very high type of character, courage, and intellectual integrity.

The MS. of Mr. Dodd was handed to me by himself, and I recall with a pathetic interest his smile of appreciative gratitude as I received it, and gave him my earnest assurance that it should be printed, and that the world would be made acquainted with his experiments and their results.

Mr. Dodd was the residuary legatee of his father, and his own will made during his last sickness, appointed me as his executor. My daughter was made his sole heir, with two exceptions; small amounts in favor of his assistants—Jeb Jobson and Andrew Clarke were mentioned in his will—and these sums have been paid by myself to each.

A series of extraordinary misfortunes, for which I am myself measurably to blame, resulted in the complete disappearance of the fortune inherited by my daughter. Her own death and that of my wife, following upon this disaster, though in no way connected with it, obliterated—and here again I admit a very grievous culpability—the remembrance of the MS. of Mr. Dodd and my own promises as to its publication.

I found the MS. of Mr. Dodd carefully wrapped up at the bottom of a trunk of papers, and confess that I opened the package it formed with a bitter sense of self-reproach. Mr. Dodd had expected to publish this paper in New York, and had requested that it should be forwarded to that city. I have at last complied with his wishes, and the MS. leaves my hands, absolutely unchanged, consigned through the kind intervention of a friend, to a publishing house in that western metropolis. I am unable to add anything more to this statement, which, in itself, I fear conveys considerable censure to the undersigned.

August Bixby Dodan.

* * * * *

Note by the Editor.

The MS. alluded to by Mr. Dodan in the preceding paragraphs was safely brought to New York in 1900, and after a very careful examination, repeatedly rejected by the prominent publishers to whom it was submitted.

Through a peculiar accident connected with some negotiations pertaining to a scientific work, contemplated by the writer, the MS. came into his hands, and he has been encouraged to publish it, influenced by the favorable comments of friends upon its intrinsic interest. He also has added to the work as an appendix, which cannot fail to attract the attention of many, the views of the great astronomer Schiaparelli upon the present physical condition of Mars, being the reproduction of an article by that distinguished observer translated from *Nature et Arte* for February, 1893, by Prof. William H. Pickering and published in the Annual Report of the Board of Regents of the Smithsonian Institution for 1894, published here by permission of "Astronomy and Astro-Physics," in which journal it first appeared in Vol. XIII., numbers 8 and 9, for October and November, 1894. In this report also appeared Schiaparelli's Map of Mars in 1888, which the Editor has not reproduced in this connection.

The introduction to-day of the wireless telegraphy, assuming a daily increasing importance, furnishes some reasonable hope that the marvellous statements given in Mr. Dodd's narrative may be more widely verified in the future, and point the way to a realization of the daring and thrilling conception of interplanetary communication.

THE PLANET MARS

BY GIOVANNI SCHIAPARELLI.

Many of the first astronomers who studied Mars with the telescope had noted on the outline of its disk two brilliant white spots of rounded form and of variable size. In process of time it was observed that while the ordinary spots upon Mars were displaced rapidly in consequence of its daily rotation, changing in a few hours both their position and their perspective, the two white spots remained sensibly motionless at their posts. It was concluded rightly from this that they must occupy the poles of rotation of the planet, or at least must be found very near to them. Consequently they were given the name of polar caps or spots. And not without reason is it conjectured that these represent upon Mars that immense mass of snow and ice which still to-day prevents navigators from reaching the poles of the earth. We are led to this conclusion not only by the analogy of aspect and of place, but also by another important observation....

As things stand, it is manifest that if the above-mentioned white polar spots of Mars represent snow and ice they should continue to decrease in size with the approach of summer in those places and increase during the winter. Now this very fact is observed in the most evident manner. In the second half of the year 1892 the southern polar cap was in full view; during that interval, and especially in the months of July and August, its rapid diminution from week to week was very evident even to those observing with common telescopes. This snow (for we may well call it so), which in the beginning reached as far as latitude 70 degrees and formed a cap of over 2,000 kilometers (1,200 miles) in diameter, progressively diminished, so that two or three months later little more of it remained than an area of perhaps 300 kilometers (180 miles) at the most, and still less was seen in the last days of 1892. In these months the southern hemisphere of Mars had its summer, the summer solstice occurring upon October 13. Correspondingly the mass of snow surrounding the northern pole should have increased; but this fact was not observable, since that pole was situated in the hemisphere of Mars which was opposite to that facing the earth. The melting of the northern snow was seen in its turn in the years 1882, 1884 and 1886.

These observations of the alternate increase and decrease of the polar snows are easily made even with telescopes of moderate power, but they become much more interesting and instructive when we can follow assiduously the changes in their more minute particulars, using larger instruments. The snowy regions are then seen to be successively notched at their edges; black holes and huge fissures are formed in their interiors; great isolated pieces many miles in extent stand out from the principal mass and, dissolving, disappear a little later. In short, the same divisions and movements of these icy fields present themselves to us at a glance that occur during the summer of our own arctic regions, according to the descriptions of explorers.

The southern snow, however, presents this peculiarity: The center of its irregularly rounded figure does not coincide exactly with the pole, but is situated at another point, which is nearly always the same, and is distant from the pole about 300 kilometers (180 miles) in the direction of the Mare Erythraeum. From this we conclude that when the area of the snow is reduced to its smallest extent the south pole of Mars is uncovered, and therefore, perhaps, the problem of reaching it upon this planet is easier than upon the earth. The southern snow is in the midst of a huge dark spot, which with its branches occupies nearly one-third of the whole surface of Mars, and is supposed to represent its principal ocean. Hence the analogy with our arctic and antarctic snows may be said to be complete, and especially so with the antarctic one.

The mass of the northern snow cap of Mars is, on the other hand, centered almost exactly upon its pole. It is located in a region of yellow color, which we are accustomed to consider as representing the continent of the planet. From this arises a singular phenomenon which has no analogy upon the earth. At the melting of the snows accumulated at that pole during the long night of ten months and more the liquid mass produced in that operation is diffused around the circumference of the snowy region, converting a large zone of surrounding land into a temporary sea and filling all the lower regions. This produces a gigantic inundation, which has led some observers to suppose the existence of another ocean in those parts, but which does not really exist in that place, at least as a permanent sea. We see then (the last opportunity was in 1884) the white spot of the snow surrounded by a dark zone, which follows its perimeter in its progressive diminution, upon a circumference ever more and more narrow. The outer part of this zone branches out into dark lines, which occupy all the surrounding region, and seem to be distributary canals by which the liquid mass may return to its natural position. This produces in these regions very extensive lakes, such as that designated upon the map by the name of Lacus Hyperboreus; the neighboring interior sea called Mare Acidalium becomes more black and more conspicuous. And it is to be remembered as a very probable thing that the flowing of this melted snow is the cause which determines principally the hydrographic state of the planet and the variations that are periodically observed in its aspect. Something similar would be seen upon the earth if one of our poles came to be located suddenly in the center of Asia or of Africa. As things stand at present, we may find a miniature image of these conditions in the flooding that is observed in our streams at the melting of the Alpine snows.

Travellers in the arctic regions have frequent occasion to observe how the state of the polar ice at the beginning of the summer, and even at the beginning of July, is always very unfavorable to their progress. The best season for exploration is in the month of August, and September is the month in which the trouble from ice is the least. Thus in September our Alps are usually more practicable than at any other season. And the reason for it is clear—the melting of the snow requires time; a high temperature is not sufficient; it is necessary that it should continue, and its effect will be so much the greater, as it is the more prolonged. Thus, if we could slow down the course of our season so that each month should last sixty days instead of thirty, in the summer, in such a lengthened condition, the melting of the ice would progress much further, and perhaps it would not be an exaggeration to say that the polar cap at the end of the warm season would be entirely destroyed. But one cannot doubt, in such a case, that the fixed portion of such a cap would be reduced to a much smaller size, than we see it to-day. Now, this is exactly what happens to Mars. The long year, nearly double our own, permits the ice to accumulate during the polar night of ten or twelve months, so as to descend in the form of a continuous layer as far as parallel 70 degrees, or even farther. But in the day which follows, of twelve or ten months, the sun has time to melt all, or nearly all, of the snow of recent formation, reducing it to such a small area that it seems to us no more than a very white point. And perhaps this snow is entirely destroyed; but of this there is at present no satisfactory observation.

Other white spots of a transitory character and of a less regular arrangement are formed in the southern hemisphere upon the islands near the pole, and also in the opposite hemisphere whitish regions appear at times surrounding the north pole and reaching to 50 degrees and 55 degrees of latitude. They are, perhaps, transitory snows, similar to those which are observed in our latitudes. But also in the torrid zone of Mars are seen some very small white spots more or less persistent; among others one was seen by me in three consecutive oppositions (1877-1882) at the point indicated upon our chart by longitude 268 degrees and latitude 16 degrees north. Perhaps we may be permitted to imagine in this place the existence of a mountain capable of supporting extensive ice fields. The existence of such a mountain has also been suggested by some recent observers upon other grounds.

As has been stated, the polar snows of Mars prove in an incontrovertible manner that this planet, like the earth, is surrounded by an atmosphere capable of transporting vapor, from one place to another. These snows are, in fact, precipitations of vapor, condensed by the cold, and carried with it successively. How carried with it if not by atmospheric movement? The existence of an atmosphere charged with vapor has been confirmed also by spectroscopic observations, principally those of Vogel, according to which this atmosphere must be of a composition differing little from our own, and above all, very rich in aqueous vapor. This is a fact of the highest importance because from it we can rightly affirm with much probability that to water and to no other liquid is due the seas of Mars and its polar snows. When this conclusion is assured beyond all doubt another one may be derived from it of not less importance—that the temperature of the Arean climate notwithstanding the greater distance of that planet from the sun, is of the same order as the temperature of the terrestrial one. Because, if it were true, as has been supposed by some investigators, that the temperature of Mars was on the average very low (from 50 degrees to 60 degrees below zero), it would not be possible for water vapor to be an important element in the atmosphere of that planet nor could Water be an important factor in its physical changes, but would give place to carbonic acid, or to some other liquid whose freezing point was much lower.

The elements of the meteorology of Mars seem, then, to have a close analogy to those of the earth. But there are not lacking, as might be expected, causes of dissimilarity. From circumstances of the smallest moment nature brings forth an infinite variety in its operations. Of the greatest influence must be different arrangement of the seas and the continents upon Mars and upon the earth, regarding which a glance at the map will say more than would be possible in many words. We have already emphasized the fact of the extraordinary periodical flood, which at every revolution of Mars inundates the northern polar region at the melting of the snow. Let us now add that this inundation is spread out to a great distance by means of a network of canals, perhaps constituting the principal mechanism (if not the only one) by which water (and with it organic life) may be diffused over the arid surface of the planet. Because on Mars it rains very rarely, or perhaps even it does not rain at all. And this is the proof.

Let us carry ourselves in imagination into celestial space, to a point so distant from the earth that we may embrace it all at a single glance. He would be greatly in error who had expected to see reproduced there upon a great scale the image of our continents with their gulfs and islands and with the seas that surround them which are seen upon our artificial globes. Then without doubt the known forms or parts of them would be seen to appear under a vaporous veil, but a great part (perhaps one-half) of the surface would be rendered invisible by the immense fields of cloud, continually varying in density, in form, and in extent. Such a hindrance, most frequent and continuous in the polar regions, would still impede nearly half the time the view of the temperate zones, distributing itself in capricious and ever varying configurations. The seas of the torrid zone would be seen to be arranged in long parallel layers, corresponding to the zone of the equatorial and tropical calms. For an observer placed upon the moon the study of our geography would not be so simple an undertaking as one might at first imagine.

There is nothing of this sort in Mars. In every climate and under every zone its atmosphere is nearly perpetually clear and sufficiently transparent to permit one to recognize at any moment whatever the contours of the seas and continents, and, more than that, even the minor configurations. Not indeed that vapors of a certain degree of opacity are lacking, but they offer very little impediment to the study of the topography of the planet. Here and there we see appear from time to time a few whitish spots, changing their position and their form, rarely extending over a very wide area. They frequent by preference a few regions, such as the islands of the Mare Australe, and on the continents the regions designated on the map with the names of Elysium and Tempe. Their brilliancy generally diminishes and disappears at the meridian hour of the place, and is re-enforced in the morning and evening with very marked variations. It is possible that they may be layers of clouds because the upper portions of terrestrial clouds where they are illuminated by the sun appear white. But various observations lead us to think that we are dealing rather with a thin veil of fog instead of a true nimbus cloud, carrying storms and rain. Indeed, it may be merely a temporary condensation of vapor under the form of dew or hoar frost.

Accordingly, as far as we may be permitted to argue from the observed facts, the climate of Mars must resemble that of a clear day upon a high mountain. By day a very strong solar radiation, hardly mitigated at all by mist or vapor; by night a copious radiation from the soil toward celestial space, and because of that a very marked refrigeration. Hence a climate of extremes, and great changes of temperature from day to night, and from one season to another. And as on the earth at altitudes of 5,000 and 6,000 meters (17,000 to 20,000 feet) the vapor of the atmosphere is condensed only into the solid form, producing those whitish masses of suspended crystals which we call cirrus clouds, so in the atmosphere of Mars it would be rarely possible (or would even be impossible) to find collections of cloud capable of producing rain of any consequence. The variation of the temperature from one season to another would be notably increased by their long duration, and thus we can understand the great freezing and melting of the snow which is renewed in turn at the poles at each complete revolution of the planet around the sun.

As our chart demonstrates, in its general topography Mars does not present any analogy with the earth. A third of its surface is occupied by the great Mare Australe, which is strewn with many islands, and the continents are cut up by gulfs, and ramifications of various forms. To the general water system belongs an entire series of small internal seas, of which the Hadriacum and the Tyrrhenum communicate with it by wide mouths, whilst the Cimmerium, the Sirenum, and the Solis Lacus are connected with it only by means of narrow canals. We shall notice in the first four a parallel arrangement, which certainly is not accidental, as also not without reason is the corresponding position of the peninsulas of Ausonia, Hesperia, and Atlantis. The color of the seas of Mars is generally brown, mixed with gray, but not always of equal intensity in all places, nor is it the same in the same place at all times. From an absolute black it may descend to a light-gray or to an ash color. Such a diversity of colors may have its origin in various causes, and is not without analogy also upon the earth, where it is noted that the seas of the warm zone are usually much darker than those nearer the pole. The water of the Baltic, for example, has a light, muddy color that is not observed in the Mediterranean. And thus in the seas of Mars we see the color become darker when the sun approaches their zenith, and summer begins to rule in that region.

All of the remainder of the planet, as far as the north pole is occupied by the mass of the continents, in which, save in a few areas of relatively small extent, an orange color predominates, which sometimes reaches a dark red tint, and in others descends to yellow and white. The variety in this coloring is in part of meteorological origin, in part it may depend on the diverse nature of the soil, but upon its real cause it is not as yet possible to frame any very well grounded hypothesis. Nevertheless, the cause of this predominance of the red and yellow tints upon the surface of ancient Pyrois is well known.[A] Some have thought to attribute this coloring to the atmosphere of Mars, through which the surface of the planet might be seen colored, as any terrestrial object becomes red when seen through red glass. But many facts are opposed to this idea, among others that the polar snows appear always of the purest white, although the rays of light derived from them traverse twice the atmosphere of Mars under great obliquity. We must then conclude that the Arean continents appear red and yellow because they are so in fact.

Besides these dark and light regions, which we have described as seas and continents, and of whose nature there is at present scarcely left any room for doubt, some others exist, truly of small extent, of an amphibious nature, which sometimes appear yellowish like the continents, and are sometimes clothed in brown (even black in certain cases), and assume the appearance of seas, whilst in other cases their color is intermediate in tint, and leaves us in doubt to which class of regions they may belong. Thus all the islands scattered through the Mare Australe and the Mare Erythræum belong to this category; so, too, the long peninsula called Deucalionis Regio and Pyrrhae Regio, and in the vicinity of the Mare Acidalium the regions designated by the names of Baltia and Nerigos. The most natural idea, and the one to which we should be led by analogy, is to suppose these regions to represent huge swamps, in which the variation in depth of the water produces the diversity of colors. Yellow would predominate in those parts where the depth of the liquid layer was reduced to little or nothing, and brown, more or less dark, in those places where the water was sufficiently deep to absorb more light and to render the bottom more or less invisible. That the water of the sea, or any other deep and transparent water, seen from above, appears more dark the greater the depth of the liquid stratum, and that the land in comparison with it appears bright under the solar illumination, is known and confirmed by certain physical reasons. The traveler in the Alps often has occasion to convince himself of it, seeing from the summits the deep lakes with which the region is strewn extending under his feet as black as ink, whilst in contrast with them even the blackest rocks illumined by the sunlight appeared brilliant.[B]

Not without reason, then, have we hitherto attributed to the dark spots of Mars the part of seas, and that of continents to the reddish areas which occupy nearly two-thirds of all the planet, and we shall find later other reasons which confirm this method of reasoning. The continents form in the northern hemisphere a nearly continuous mass, the only important exception being the great lake called the Mare Acidalium, of which the extent may vary according to the time, and which is connected in some way with the inundations which we have said were produced by the melting of the snow surrounding the north pole. To the system of the Mare Acidalium undoubtedly belong the temporary lake called Lacus Hyperboreus and the Lacus Niliacus. This last is ordinarily separated from the Mare Acidalium by means of an isthmus or regular dam, of which the continuity was only seen to be broken once for a short time in 1888. Other smaller dark spots are found here and there in the continental area which we may designate as lakes, but they are certainly not permanent lakes like ours, but are variable in appearance and size according to the seasons, to the point of wholly disappearing under certain circumstances. Ismenius Lacus, Lunae Lacus, Trivium Charontis, and Propontis are the most conspicuous and durable ones. There are also smaller ones, such as Lacus Moeris and Fons Juventae, which at their maximum size do not exceed 100 to 150 kilometers (60 to 90 miles) in diameter, and are among the most difficult objects upon the planet.

All the vast extent of the continents is furrowed upon every side by a network of numerous lines or fine stripes of a more or less pronounced dark color, whose aspect is very variable. These traverse the planet for long distances in regular lines that do not at all resemble the winding courses of our streams. Some of the shorter ones do not reach 500 kilometers (300 miles), others, on the other hand, extend for many thousands, occupying a quarter or sometimes even a third of a circumference of the planet. Some of these are very easy to see, especially that one which is near the extreme left-hand limit of our map and is designated by the name of Nilosyrtis. Others in turn are extremely difficult, and resemble the finest thread of spider's web drawn across the disk. They are subject also to great variations in their breadth, which may reach 200 or even 300 kilometers (120 to 180 miles) for the Nilosyrtis, whilst some are scarcely 30 kilometers (18 miles) broad.

These lines or stripes are the famous canals of Mars, of which so much has been said. As far as we have been able to observe them hitherto, they are certainly fixed configurations upon the planet. The Nilosyrtis has been seen in that place for nearly one hundred years, and some of the others for at least thirty years. Their length and arrangement are constant, or vary only between very narrow limits. Each of them always begins and ends between the same regions. But their appearance and their degree of visibility vary greatly, for all of them, from one opposition to another, and even from one week to another, and these variations do not take place simultaneously and according to the same laws for all, but in most cases happen apparently capriciously, or at least according to laws not sufficiently simple for us to be able to unravel. Often one or more become indistinct, or even wholly invisible, whilst others in their vicinity increase to the point of becoming conspicuous even in telescopes of moderate power. The first of our maps shows all those that have been seen in a long series of observations. This does not at all correspond to the appearance of Mars at any given period, because generally only a few are visible at once.[C]

Every canal (for now we shall so call them) opens at its ends either into a sea, or into a lake, or into another canal, or else into the intersection of several other canals. None of them have yet been seen cut off in the middle of the continent, remaining without beginning or without end. This fact is of the highest importance. The canals may intersect among themselves at all possible angles, but by preference they converge toward the small spots to which we have given the name of lakes. For example, seven are seen to converge in Lacus Phoenicis, eight in Trivium Charontis, six in Lunae Lacus, and six in Ismenius Lacus.

The normal appearance of a canal is that of a nearly uniform stripe, black, or at least of a dark color, similar to that of the seas, in which the regularity of its general course does not exclude small variations in its breadth and small sinuosities in its two sides. Often it happens that such a dark line opening out upon the sea is enlarged into the form of a trumpet, forming a huge bay, similar to the estuaries of certain terrestrial streams. The Margaritifer Sinus, the Aonius Sinus, the Aurorae Sinus, and the two horns of the Sabæus Sinus are thus formed, at the mouths of one or more canals, opening into the Mare Erythraeum or into the Mare Australe. The largest example of such a gulf is the Syrtis Major, formed by the vast mouth of the Nilosyrtis, so called. This gulf is not less than 1,800 kilometers (1,100 miles) in breadth, and attains nearly the same depth in a longitudinal direction. Its surface is little less than that of the Bay of Bengal. In this case we see clearly the dark surface of the sea continued without apparent interruption into that canal. Inasmuch as the surfaces called seas are truly a liquid expanse, we cannot doubt that the canals are a simple prolongation of them, crossing the yellow areas or continents.

Of the remainder, that the lines called canals are truly great furrows or depressions in the surface of the planet, destined for the passage of the liquid mass and constituting for it a true hydrographic system, is demonstrated by the phenomena which are observed during the melting of the northern snows. We have already remarked that at the time of melting they appear surrounded by a dark zone, forming a species of temporary sea. At that time the canals of the surrounding region become blacker and wider, increasing to the point of converting at a certain time all of the yellow region comprised between the edge of the snow and the parallel of 60 degrees north latitude into numerous islands of small extent. Such a state of things does not cease until the snow, reduced to its minimum area, ceases to melt. Then the breadth of the canals diminishes, the temporary sea disappears, and the yellow region again returns to its former area. The different phases of these vast phenomena are renewed at each return of the seasons, and we were able to observe them in all their particulars very easily during the oppositions of 1882, 1884, and 1886, when the planet presented its northern pole to terrestrial spectators. The most natural and the most simple interpretation is that to which we have referred, of a great inundation produced by the melting of the snows; it is entirely logical and is sustained by evident analogy with terrestrial phenomena. We conclude, therefore, that the canals are such in fact and not only in name. The network formed by these was probably determined in its origin in the geological state of the planet, and has come to be slowly elaborated in the course of centuries. It is not necessary to suppose them the work of intelligent beings, and, notwithstanding the almost geometrical appearance of all of their system, we are now inclined to believe them to be produced by the evolution of the planet, just as on the earth we have the English Channel and the channel of Mozambique.

It would be a problem not less curious than complicated and difficult to study the system of this immense stream of water, upon which perhaps depends principally the organic life upon the planet, if organic life is found there. The variations of their appearance demonstrated that this system is not constant. When they become displaced or their outlines become doubtful and ill defined, it is fair to suppose that the water is getting low or is even entirely dried up. Then, in place of the canals there remains either nothing or at most stripes of yellowish color differing little from the surrounding background. Sometimes they take on a nebulous appearance, for which at present it is not possible to assign a reason. At other times true enlargements are produced, expanding to 100, 200 or more kilometers (60 to 120 miles) in breadth, and this sometimes happens for canals very far from the north pole, according to laws which are unknown. This occurred in Hydaspes in 1864, in Simois in 1879, in Ackeron in 1884, and in Triton in 1888. The diligent and minute study of the transformations of each canal may lead later to a knowledge of the causes of these effects.

But the most surprising phenomenon pertaining to the canals of Mars is their germination, which seems to occur principally in the months which precede and in those which follow the great northern inundation—at about the times of the equinoxes. In consequence of a rapid process, which certainly lasts at most a few days, or even perhaps, only a few hours, and of which it has not yet been possible to determine the particulars with certainty, a given canal changes its appearance and is found transformed through all its length into two lines or uniform stripes more or less parallel to one another, and which run straight and equal with the exact geometrical precision of the two rails of a railroad. But this exact course is the only point of resemblance with the rails, because in dimensions there is no comparison possible, as it is easy to imagine. These two lines follow very nearly the direction of the original canal and end in the place where it ended. One of these is often superposed as exactly as possible upon the former line, the other being drawn anew; but in this case the original line loses all the small irregularities and curvature that it may have originally possessed. But it also happens that both the lines may occupy opposite sides of the' former canal and be located upon entirely new ground. The distance between the two lines differs in different germinations and varies from 600 kilometers (360 miles) and more down to the smallest limit at which two lines may appear separated in large visual telescopes—less than at intervals of 50 kilometers (30 miles). The breadth of the stripes themselves may range from the limit of visibility, which we may suppose to be 30 kilometers (18 miles), up to more than 100 kilometers (60 miles). The color of the two lines varies from black to a light red, which can hardly be distinguished from the general yellow background of the continental surface. The space between is for the most part yellow, but in many cases appears whitish. The gemination is not necessarily confined only to the canals, but tends to be produced also in the lakes. Often one of these is seen transformed into two short, broad, dark lines parallel to one another and traversed by a yellow line. In these cases the gemination is naturally short and does not exceed the limits of the original lake.

The gemination is not shown by all at the same time, but when the season is at hand it begins to be produced here and there, in an isolated, irregular manner, or at least without any easily recognizable order. In many canals (such as the Nilosyrtis, for example), the gemination is lacking entirely, or is scarcely visible. After having lasted for some months, the markings fade out gradually and disappear until another season equally favorable for their formation. Thus it happens that in certain other seasons (especially near the southern solstice of the planet) few are seen, or even none at all. In different oppositions the gemination of the same canal may present different appearances as to width, intensity, and arrangement of the two stripes; also in some cases the direction of the lines may vary, although by the smallest quantity, but still deviating by a small amount from the canal with which they are directly associated. From this important fact it is immediately understood that the gemination cannot be a fixed formation upon the surface of Mars and of a geographical character like the canals. The second of our maps will give an approximate idea of the appearance which these singular formations present. It contains all the geminations observed since 1882 up to the present time. In examining it it is necessary to bear in mind that not all of these appearances were simultaneous, and consequently that the map does not represent the condition of Mars at any given period; it is only a sort of topographical register of the observations made of this phenomenon at different times.[D]

The observation of the gemination is one of the greatest difficulty, and can only be made by an eye well practiced in such work, added to a telescope of accurate construction and of great power. This explains why it is that it was not seen before 1882. In the ten years that have transpired since that time, it has been seen and described at eight or ten observatories. Nevertheless, some still deny that these phenomena are real, and tax with illusion (or even imposture) those who declare that they have observed it.

Their singular aspect, and their being drawn with absolute geometrical precision, as if they were the work of rule or compass, has led some to see in them the work of intelligent beings, inhabitants of the planet. I am very careful not to combat this supposition, which includes nothing impossible. (Io mi guarderò bene dal combattere questa supposizione, la quale nulla include d'impossibile.) But it will be noticed that in any case the gemination cannot be a work of permanent character, it being certain that in a given instance it may change its appearance and dimensions from one season to another. If we should assume such a work, a certain variability would not be excluded from it; for example, extensive agricultural labor and irrigation upon a large scale. Let us add, further, that the intervention of intelligent beings might explain the geometrical appearance of the gemination, but it is not at all necessary for such a purpose. The geometry of nature is manifested in many other facts from which are excluded the idea of any artificial labor whatever. The perfect spheroids of the heavenly bodies and the ring of Saturn were not constructed in a turning lathe, and not with compasses has Iris described within the clouds her beautiful and regular arch. And what shall we say of the infinite variety of those exquisite and regular polyhedrons in which the world of crystals is so rich? In the organic world, also, is not that geometry most wonderful which presides over the distribution of the foliage upon certain plants, which orders the nearly symmetrical, star-like figures of the flowers of the field, as well as of the sea, and which produces in the shell such an exquisite conical spiral that excels the most beautiful masterpieces of Gothic architecture? In all these objects the geometrical form is the simple and necessary consequence of the principles and laws which govern the physical and physiological world. That these principles and these laws are but an indication of a higher intelligent Power we may admit, but this has nothing to do with the present argument.

Having regard, then, for the principle that in the explanation of natural phenomena it is universally agreed to begin with the simplest suppositions, the first hypotheses of the nature and cause of the geminations have for the most part put in operation only the laws of inorganic nature. Thus, the gemination is supposed to be due either to the effects of light in the atmosphere of Mars, or to optical illusions produced by vapors in various manners, or to glacial phenomena of a perpetual winter, to which it is known all the planets will be condemned, or to double cracks in its surface, or to single cracks of which the images are doubled by the effect of smoke issuing in long lines and blown laterally by the wind. The examination of these ingenious suppositions leads us to conclude that none of them seem to correspond entirely with the observed facts, either in whole or in part. Some of these hypotheses would not have been proposed had their authors been able to examine the geminations with their own eyes. Since some of these may ask me directly, "Can you suggest anything better?" I must reply candidly, "No."

It would be far more easy if we were willing to introduce the forces pertaining to organic nature. Here the field of plausible supposition is immense, being capable of making an infinite number of combinations capable of satisfying the appearances even with the smallest and simplest means. Changes of vegetation over a vast area, and the production of animals, also very small, but in enormous multitudes, may well be rendered visible at such a distance. An observer placed in the moon would be able to see such an appearance at the times in which agricultural operations are carried out upon one vast plain—the seed-time and the gathering of the harvest. In such a manner also would the flowers of the plants of the great steppes of Europe and Asia be rendered visible at the distance of Mars—by a variety of coloring. A similar system of operations produced in that planet may thus certainly be rendered visible to us. But how difficult for the Lunarians and the Areans to be able to imagine the true causes of such changes of appearance without having first at least some superficial knowledge of terrestrial nature! So also for us, who know so little of the physical state of Mars, and nothing of its organic world, the great liberty of possible supposition renders arbitrary all explanations of this sort and constitutes the gravest obstacle to the acquisition of well-founded notions. All that we may hope is that with time the uncertainty of the problem will gradually diminish, demonstrating if not what the geminations are, at least what they cannot be. We may also confide a little in what Galileo called "the courtesy of nature," thanks to which a ray of light from an unexpected source will sometimes illuminate an investigation at first believed inaccessible to our speculations, and of which we have a beautiful example in celestial chemistry. Let us therefore hope and study.

FOOTNOTES:

[Footnote A: Pyrois I take to be some terrestrial region, although I have not been able to find any translation of the name.—Translator.]

[Footnote B: This observation of the dark color which deep water exhibits when seen from above is found already noted by the first author of antique memory, for in the Iliad (verses 770-771 of Book V) it is described how "the sentinel from the high sentry box extends his glance over the wine-colored sea, [Greek: *oinopa phonton*]." In the version of Monti the adjective indicating the color is lost.]

[Footnote C: In a footnote the author refers to a drawing of Mars made by himself, September 15, 1892, and says, ... "At the top of the disk the Mare Erythraeum and the Mare Australe appear divided by a great curved peninsula, shaped like a sickle, producing an unusual appearance in the area called Deucalionis Regio, which was prolonged that year so as to reach the islands of Noachis and Argyre. This region forms with them a continuous whole, but with faint traces of separation occurring here and there in a length of nearly 6,000 kilometers (4,000 miles). Its color, much less brilliant than that of the continents, was a mixture of their yellow with the brownish gray of the neighboring seas." The interesting feature of this note is the remark that it was an unusual appearance, the region referred to being that in which the central branch of the fork of the Y appeared. Since no such branch was conspicuously visible this year, it would therefore seem from the above that it was the opposition of 1892 that was peculiar, and not the present one.—Translator.]

[Footnote D: This map may be found also in La Planète Mars, by Flammarion, page 44.—Translator.]

CPSIA information can be obtained
at www.ICGtesting.com
Printed in the USA
LVHW031104170821
695475LV00003B/636

9 789354 849121